"What's  to me?"

There was d... ...my life I've felt calm and secure, and how you've drawn me through the doorway of another world!"

"You are quite the little coward," Alex said cuttingly.

"Am I?" She was shaking. "Because I'm totally unprepared for loving you?"

"Ah, you've said it." His vibrant voice had a goading tone. "You don't seem to appreciate that you've got me nearly out of my mind. Why don't I ask you what right you have to turn my life upside down? I was quite happy before. There was none of this terrible urgency for a woman. There have been other beautiful girls in my life—but that seems like light-years ago. You are aware that you are my woman."

His arms closed around her as his mouth covered hers....

Margaret Way takes great pleasure in her work and works hard at her pleasure. She enjoys tearing off to the beach with her family on weekends, loves haunting galleries and auctions and is completely given over to French champagne "for every possible joyous occasion." Her home, perched high on a hill overlooking Brisbane, Australia, is her haven. She started writing when her son was a baby, and now she finds there is no better way to spend her time.

Books by Margaret Way

HARLEQUIN ROMANCE

HARLEQUIN PRESENTS

These books may be available at your local bookseller.

Don't miss any of our special offers. Write to us at the following address for information on our newest releases.

Harlequin Reader Service
901 Fuhrmann Blvd., P.O. Box 1397, Buffalo, NY 14240
Canadian address: P.O. Box 603,
Fort Erie, Ont. L2A 5X3

Innocent
in Eden
Margaret Way

Harlequin Books

TORONTO • NEW YORK • LONDON
AMSTERDAM • PARIS • SYDNEY • HAMBURG
STOCKHOLM • ATHENS • TOKYO • MILAN

Original hardcover edition published in 1986
by Mills & Boon Limited

ISBN 0-373-02820-2

Harlequin Romance first edition February 1987

Printed in U.S.A.

CHAPTER ONE

A THOUSAND feet above the city streets, the views of Sydney and its harbour were so majestic and immense that visitors to the revolving restaurant were usually dazzled by the panoramic spectacle, but not Liz Stoddart. Liz had the reputation for being single-minded and she was mostly at pains to live up to it. While everyone else's gaze migrated to the magic, Liz spared it not a glance. She forged ahead fearlessly as one is supposed to in life.

'Splendid, splendid!' she cried merrily and gave Jane, her young English assistant, exactly the same sort of prod Jane had endured for years at Sports. 'Sit there, dear.'

'Surely you'd like the window seat?'

Jane was prodded again for her girlish dithering.

'There!' Liz repeated in the tone of one who rarely failed to get her way.

'Do it, Jane,' Perry Wyndham urged, humour eclipsing a quiver of irritability. Perry, a highly successful expatriate film-director, was recovering from a bad case of jet-lag.

'I live to please.' Jane slid in beside him. 'It's so clear one can see the Blue Mountains.'

'So you *can*!' Liz spun her dark-helmeted head. 'You know why they're so outstandingly blue, don't you, Jane?'

'I understood it was the high oil content in the trees and shrubs.'

'And a trick of height and distance and temperature. The oil vapour scatters the light or some such thing.

5

That's the cause of those marvellous blue rays. The early settlers never called them anything else but the Blue Mountains.'

'They're very beautiful!' Jane, the nature-lover, breathed, and on reflection came to the conclusion, 'They must have been a frightful challenge to cross.'

'Easier if a few aborigines had pointed the way,' Perry suggested sardonically, 'but black and white weren't on the best of terms as will be amply demonstrated in our movie. *If* it ever gets off the ground.'

'Leave it to me, dear boy,' Liz said confidently. 'In any case we won't be dealing with our own aboriginal people but the kanakas. Natives from the Solomons, the New Hebrides and parts of New Guinea who worked our cotton and sugar plantations. More than 50,000 were landed by the turn of the century.'

'Blackbirded, don't you mean?' Bryan Rowland, the scriptwriter, murmured laconically. 'In theory the poor devils were voluntary labour. In practice a lot of them were kidnapped from their island homes and forced to work the fields. Small wonder a few of them went crazed.'

'When was it outlawed again?' Jane asked.

'1904.' Liz had researched the period exhaustively. 'The British Government followed suit in Fiji a few years later. It all started because it was thought no white man could work the fields in the tropical heat. Of course they later did, very successfully. They were exciting, violent times and it will come across in our film. Our first settlers *had* to be ruthless, determined men. How else could they have pioneered a wild continent—not only pioneered it, conquered it? Another world, so different from anything they were used to. Consider *that*! Our great pioneers were men of passion. So is our hero. His is a story of great power and determination——'

'And destruction,' Jane added quietly.

'Lots of *drama*!' Liz agreed enthusiastically. 'Oh, it's marvellous to have you here, Perry. I know we're going to do great things together. It's especially exciting the breakthrough of women. We're numbered among the top producers now. Of course it had to be. Women can't live their lives in closets and kitchens. Our immense talents have to be recognised.'

'Apparently. Is that it, Liz?' Bryan asked.

'*No*, Bryan. I'm sick of—yes, sick of the way we women are ridiculed and abused.'

'I'd hate to try and ridicule you.' Bryan turned his head to study Liz's Junoesque frame.

'Look here, Bryan . . .'

'He's joking, Liz,' Jane intervened soothingly. 'Always joking.'

'It's not too pleasant.'

'Sorry, old girl.' Bryan patted Liz's hand. 'All it means is I love you. Didn't I give you your first break?'

'So you did,' Liz nodded, not altogether gratefully. 'Without ever knowing what I did.'

'What was the smog like in Los Angeles?' Jane quickly asked Perry.

'A curse.' He lifted his hand languidly and took a strand of Jane's blonde hair between his fingers. 'A beautiful colour. Dare I ask if it's real?'

'Of course it's *real*!' Liz snorted. 'Anyone could see Jane's a natural blonde.'

'She has dark brows and lashes.'

'It runs in the family,' Jane pointed out.

'A striking combination. Blonde hair, green eyes and those long dark lashes. A skin like cream.'

'Leave Jane alone, Perry,' Liz ordered. 'He's been married twice, dear.'

'As much as that?' Perry, fortyish, attractively jaded, gave Jane a wry look. 'It's difficult when one is surrounded by beautiful women.'

'The worse thing you ever did was to leave us,' Liz said decisively.

'So what's money?' Bryan asked. 'Fame?'

'Does it matter so much when you're not doing what you *want* to do?' Liz challenged.

'Thank God, here's the waiter.' Bryan signalled expertly with his hand.

'This must be one of the great sights of the world,' he mused, after they had all ordered. 'I've missed it. You have no idea.'

'We knew you weren't a cold fish, darling.' Liz nodded her dark head approvingly. 'Now I don't want to intrude on the old nostalgia but we do have a few things to discuss and time is of the essence. Perhaps next time, Jane, you won't book us in to the highest building in the Southern Hemisphere. The competition is too strong.'

'Blue sky, blue sea and all that golden sunlight. Sydney is a pretty high-powered place these days.'

'Blooming.' Liz allowed her brilliant, dark eyes to rove from the Botanic Gardens to the soaring white sails of the Opera House and on to the Harbour Bridge. 'Of course it's the harbour that makes Sydney such a showplace. Being a Melburian——'

'Please, *don't*,' Bryan pleaded. 'We all know you're an old Melburian, dear. Though how such a sober city produced you . . .'

'It produces all the best people.'

'Not to mention the riff-raff.'

Jane and Perry paid little attention. Liz and Bryan would bicker for hours without taking breath. A lot of people in the business found this wearing but no one could deny either of them their prodigious talents. A top New York critic had gone into raves about Liz's last film and this more than anything had persuaded Perry to return home. For months now they had been discussing the filming of an old Queensland classic, *Sugar King*, based on the life and times of Black Jack McGovern, the most famous and flamboyant of the early sugar barons. No film-maker could ask for a more glorious location. Tropical North Queensland was a veritable Garden of Eden and if the present McGovern would only be good enough to allow them the run of the historic McGovern plantation, Monteverdi, the whole project would be as good as in the can.

'What's this McGovern like?' Perry asked, after a soothing draught of wine.

'Very *rich*!' Liz declared enthusiastically. 'Helpful when we're on such a small budget. They live splendidly in an incredible Renaissance villa. An Anglo-Italian family. The matriarch is Italian at any rate. A real old tartar according to my sources. She lives on the estate.'

'Show me a woman and I'll show you trouble,' Bryan mourned.

'They do lend colour.' Perry was idly admiring the effect of the sunlight on Jane's beautiful hair.

'Apparently she's a terrible snob,' Liz continued. 'McGovern himself is said to exude wealth and power. My spies tell me he's incredibly handsome and sexy to boot.'

'Lucky devil!' Bryan breathed.

'What I can't understand,' Jane said, 'is how the author escaped legal action. The book is too close to fact for comfort. The McGoverns would be within their rights to object to the whole thing.'

'There's a penalty for our sins,' Bryan said gloomily.

'And darling, you have my deepest sympathy,' Liz told him. 'Whatever the problems we'll get around them. That's if we're cunning.'

'Sounds like we might need a re-write, Bryan,' Perry remarked drily. 'As Jane has pointed out it's remarkably close to McGovern's own life.'

'A ready-made drama. Armstrong scarcely had to think up a thing. Hero second son of a distinguished Scottish family. Goes off adventuring at twenty. Marries an Italian Contessa, carries her off to a colonial jungle on the other side of the world. Builds her a replica of her own ancestral home to keep her happy. Eventually imports an English governess of good family to educate his children. Governess thrives on the new life as any intrepid Englishwoman would. Contessa has a nervous breakdown. Hero and governess fall in love. Contessa mysteriously disappears from the face of the earth. Lots of theories— murdered by a crazed kanaka, taken by a crocodile, drowned. McGovern marries governess. Scandal upon scandal. It really happened before Armstrong put it together in novel form.'

'Spicy, heh?' Liz chuckled. 'And we have to get it up there on the big screen. Anyway it was all so long ago I expect everyone has forgotten.'

'People never forget loose living,' Bryan warned her. 'Does Noosa Beach ring a bell?'

'Go to hell, Bryan,' Liz said crossly, reddening slightly beneath her healthy tan.

'Only if you'll guide me.'

The catch of the day arrived—the restaurant was renowned for its splendid seafood—and a temporary truce was declared.

'They must have been savage days,' Jane mused a few minutes later. 'Men who succeeded had to be like McGovern. Tough, powerful, capable of working the wilderness. It must have been ferocious hacking through virgin jungle in the intense heat.'

'Excellent stuff, isn't it?' Liz said. 'It was nothing to sit on a million acres.'

'A million acres no one knew anything about. Nothing marked on a map. Australia must have seemed like another planet to the Europeans. Flat plains like oceans, the blinding light. Everything so *different* ... the trees and the vegetation, the strange animals. The first white man must have been startled to see a kangaroo.'

'You can still be startled when they hop straight into your car,' Bryan complained. 'The poor old convicts used to say when they headed for the bush, "over the hills and to the north lies China". Poor devils! All they found was a desert.'

'Plenty more established themselves,' Liz said. 'But it must have been a grim and lonely life even for those that blazed the trails.'

'It was the introduction of kanaka labour that sparked off bitterness in the sugar lands, wasn't it?' Jane asked.

'The most bitter disputes in the colony's history,' Perry told her. 'You have a lovely voice, Jane.'

'Why, thank you.' Jane turned to smile at him.

'And a lovely smile.'

'Perry!' Liz gave him a sharp look over her glass.

'In fact, young Jane, you're not what I expected at all.'

'What *did* you expect, old boy?' Liz demanded.

Perry gave his attractive, wry smile. 'Oh, an assistant like any other. Pleasant but difficult to remember. Jane could spend the rest of her life on champagne and caviar if I took her back with me. She has that delectable English skin, excellent bones, a sexy, full-lipped mouth. She's rather like the young Jean Shrimpton, don't you think?'

'Better legs,' Bryan said appreciatively. 'Terrific legs. I saw Shrimpton at the Melbourne Cup and hers were too skinny.'

'Goodness, it's impossible not to blush,' Jane said calmly. Perry Wyndham was a very attractive man but his particular brand of charm, plus the big age difference, kept Jane serene.

'Don't go filling Jane's head with any nonsensical ideas, Perry,' Liz warned him. 'She's quite happy as she is and I couldn't do without her. She's my right hand and she's under my wing while she's in Australia. I speak to her mother on the phone.'

'She does,' Jane confirmed smilingly. 'Beneath Liz's commanding exterior beats a soft heart of gold.'

'Is there a boyfriend lurking around somewhere?' Perry asked. If Jane was immune to him, Perry was finding her more and more attractive.

'No one special.' Long dark lashes veiled her sea-green eyes.

'Remember the *two* wives, Jane.'

'What a little chum you are, Liz,' Perry said just a shade testily. 'Besides, when have I ever been a cradle-snatcher?'

' '82?' Bryan ventured.

'I'm always attracted to the wrong people.'

'Ditto.' Bryan muttered with a sidelong glance at Liz.

Liz neither heard nor saw him. 'Don't let's get off the track,' she exhorted and all but thumped the table. 'I think *Sugar King* will go over really big. A Scot, in fact, did pioneer our sugar industry. The Honorable Louis Hope, son of the Earl of Hopetoun. He migrated to Australia about the time our hero was born. Hope founded a great industry with his sugar plantation in Brisbane. He even built a mansion, Ormiston House, after the ancestral home in Scotland. He recruited kanakas as well. They all did. No gentleman was expected to labour in the fields. Fortunately it's on record McGovern treated the kanakas well. So too the Chinese he employed. He made an even greater fortune in the goldfields. In a lot of ways plantation life in Queensland closely resembled plantation life in the American South. Black labour was used in the fields and in the house. There were even Mammies for the planters' children.'

'McGovern didn't want no Mammy,' Bryan pointed out. 'He had Miss Laura Hamilton, a slim little blonde who didn't run fast enough away from the Master.'

'In that case our film might stir up a great deal of talk and family resentment,' Jane ventured. 'The public might believe it's *all* fact.'

'Don't be silly,' Liz said sharply. 'The film will have no existence outside of fiction. So Armstrong drew a little——'

'A *lot*.'

'On real life. He would never have dreamt one day someone would make a film out of it.'

'But the McGoverns are still there,' Jane said. 'So is the house. So are the old scandals.'

'Listen, dear,' Liz asked aggrievedly, 'whose side are you on?'

'Yours every time, Liz,' Jane maintained. 'I want you to be happy. I want you to make a great film. I don't want you to get involved in a legal wrangle. Important people are generally proud and they don't accept things like most people have to. They may set out to stop us.'

'The sensible thing—indeed the only thing—is to fly up there and arrange a meeting with this McGovern,' Perry said. 'There's money in it for him if he's interested. Stress the investor's angle. I've never known a rich man overlook new ways to make money.'

'What if he refuses to meet you at all?' Bryan asked with a studiously blank face.

'He won't!' Liz maintained in her usual indomitable fashion. 'It's imperative he help us.'

'Just the way you say the word!' Bryan admired.

'Shut up, Bryan,' Liz hissed, really quite irritated with Bryan. 'I don't want to twist the story around too much. That would be robbing it of its great strength. I'm sure if I can meet with Mr Alex McGovern we can arrive at an acceptable compromise.'

'Better you than me,' Bryan sighed gratefully. 'I'll be damned if I'm going to invite any punch on the nose.'

'I'll be tied up as well, Liz,' Perry told her. 'This was all your idea and a great idea it is if you can enlist the McGoverns' co-operation.'

'I'll need Jane.'

'Actually *my* plans included Jane,' Perry said.

'Your plans, my boy, will have to wait. I rely a lot on Jane's Pommy diplomacy.'

'Doesn't she ever!' Bryan seconded. 'Poor old Jane has to soothe many a ruffled feather.'

'I'd love to go!' Jane declared. 'They tell me north of Capricorn is another world.'

'It's bloody *hot!*' Bryan did not smile. 'A whole year of high summer.'

'I don't mind, Bryan,' Jane said eagerly. 'I love the sun. It's outstanding. I might find the time to see the Great Barrier Reef.'

'After we see the McGoverns,' Liz agreed indulgently. 'It won't all be poincianas and palm trees, Jane. We have to make this McGovern want to help us in every way. It's his duty to help us if he's at all patriotic. What's the use of owning a great villa if one can't billet a film crew or at least the stars? We're a young industry and we're going places.'

'That we are!' Perry seconded with a note of pride.

'Then I'll book our air tickets, shall I?'

'I think I can be ready first thing Wednesday morning,' Liz considered.

'And in case anything goes wrong,' Bryan warned Jane prophetically, 'better tell your mother.'

CHAPTER TWO

NORTH of Capricorn *was* another world, an eternal
world of cane that flowed right into town, of sugar
ships and terminals, of giant harvesters and little cane
trains, of picturesque Queensland houses standing on
stilts for all the world like South Pacific villages but
surrounded by wide verandahs decorated with intricate
wrought iron or delicate lattice work. Indian,
Moorish, whatever, they seemed far more uniquely
Australian to Jane's eyes than the traditional architecture of the Southern States. Australia in general
had been settled by British immigrants so the style of
architecture followed Home designs but somehow
Queensland had evolved a form of its own.

'White ants, dear,' Liz explained it. 'One has to
keep the floor-boards out of reach.'

'Of course!' Jane acknowledged. 'The climate is so
very different one would have to make concessions.
Look at this delicious froth of a sundress.'

'I might as well. Every male in the hotel has. What
is it about blondes? They really do turn heads. Even
plain ones rate a second glance.'

'I learnt that long ago.' Jane was standing on the little
balcony looking out. 'I love the way the timber houses
are high-set on their tall piers with planters' chairs all
around the wide verandahs. Some of the houses are very
grand indeed. The ones on acreage. But even the modest
houses have a charm of their own. The gardens are so
lush! I don't think I've ever seen so many riotously
blooming plants. And the scents! I'm nearly dizzy with it
all. It's incredibly seductive!'

'You're young.' Liz, at forty-two, yawned. 'Nature is bountiful up here, but it's wanton as well. For about nine months of the year it's paradise followed by bedlam. The monsoon season is from January to March. The Wet they call it. Only two cycles really. The Wet and the Dry. The temperature never drops low enough to make any difference to people or plants or animals. It will be hotter soon.'

'Well, it's wonderful now,' Jane said rapturously, looking up at the orchid-decked rain-forest that all but encroached on the town. 'How's the head?'

'Niggling,' Liz said. 'Flying never does agree with me.'

'What about if I ring for a pot of tea? I usually find a cup of tea works a miracle.'

'Lovely, dear.' Liz, who was lying with her eyes shut, breathed. 'I just hope I don't go troppo.'

'Shall I close the shutters?'

'You might, those.' Liz waved a hand. 'Lovely outlook, haven't we? Right over the bay. I've never seen so many colours in the sea. Aqua, green like your eyes, emerald, cobalt. It's lovely to get into such light-weight clothing.'

'I might take a walk,' Jane turned back to say. 'The sea breeze is beautiful and I want to take a closer look at all those yachts in the marina.'

'Right, dear,' Liz murmured, nicely settled. 'You really need a hat. One of those big coolie things. If you see a shop, buy one.'

Jane spent more than an hour roaming around the drowsy sun-drenched beach town. No one hurried. There was no need to. It was Lotus Land with all the signs of prosperity but none of the bustle of the key cities that served the canelands, the tobacco, minerals and timber, the cattle kings and the agricultural wealth of the hinterland. The only reason they were there at all was that it was the closest they could get to the McGovern stronghold. Even in the short time since they had arrived they had already discovered the whole district owed its prosperity to various McGovern enterprises. As a receptionist told them, 'The McGoverns own the town.'

Beautiful garden plots ran down the centre of the main street interspersed with great palms in the shapes of giant fans, Travellers Palms. Groups of people from the tourist buses were enjoying al fresco coffee amid the beautiful surroundings and Jane crossed the esplanade heading towards the marina with its impressive flotilla of motor yachts, blue-water ketches and sloops. A super sailing yacht was enjoying the bay and Jane shaded her eyes as the vision took hold of her imagination. Her father and two brothers were excellent sailors, and they would love to sail around this tropical paradise with its hundreds of magical islands and fjord-like bays. These were glorious waters and she thought about the possibility of hiring a boat and doing some exploring. To her softly dazzled eyes the place had the façade of paradise, blue sky, blue sea, majestic palms and gloriously flowering trees, and in the near distance hundreds upon hundreds of palm-fringed coral cays teeming with rainbow-coloured birds. It was incredibly lush and luxuriant and she was revelling in the steady south-easterly that was fanning her hair out and keeping the tropical air cool.

Further out in the bay the blue waters were sparkling and ruffled by the breeze but here in the marina the water was mirror-still, reflecting the myriad craft with translucent clarity. It would be a very simple matter for a dreamer to escape. The Great Barrier Reef was the largest coral conglomeration in the world and one of the great wonders of the world.

It was unthinkable she should leave this place without visiting at least one of those magical coral cays that floated like jade rings on blue crystal waters. Jane was surprised by the intensity of her emotions. She was intoxicated by the place, probably more than was good for her. Even her body felt seductive and aroused.

From the far jetty an aboriginal boy of perhaps ten was having the most marvellous time diving into the deep water and sporting like a dolphin. Jane kept her eye on him for a few minutes then when it became apparent he was well able to look after himself she began to enjoy his antics. Now that he saw her looking at him he tried even harder to entertain her and Jane waited and watched and afterwards gave him a friendly little salute and commenced her return trip to the esplanade.

She was daydreaming now, imagining herself a castaway on one of those magical islands. Of course she wouldn't be alone. The isolation of it all would be transformed by romance. She started to think who she would like to be with her. Richard Gere? Pierce Brosnan? Tom Selleck? She ran through a list of names getting sillier and sillier. She was really waiting for the right guy. He would be tall, dark and terribly attractive. A fine, fluent talker. He would be highly intelligent, naturally, full of integrity, generous and tolerant. He would have a great sense of humour which meant they would find the same things funny. He would be a softie at heart though he would never admit to it. Her family would love him because he was so darned *nice*. They would agree on all major issues but cross the occasional sword. They would give each other tremendous support and pleasure. She was really glad at twenty-two she would come to him a virgin despite enormous peer-pressure to liberate her body. Now and again she had felt a spark and indulged in her share of kisses and caresses but she had never really *cared* enough to surrender her all. Possibly she felt too powerfully about it. She had the idea sex ought to be beautiful and mysterious and at least a bit holy and not a series of careless romps after parties. Of course there remained the possibility she would meet someone utterly irresistible and pay the price of total abandonment like the passionate heroines of fiction. This was the ideal setting for some fatal seduction. Jasmine-wreathed plantations, mountain pinnacles always shrouded in mist, a fantasy world of exotica and offshore the awesomely beautiful Reef.

Jane was so spellbound by her brilliant visions she had never once turned to notice the magnificent sailing yacht she had admired in the bay coming in under power to its mooring-bay in the marina. The strong sea breeze had been against her making a wildly ornamental curtain of her ash-gold hair, now suddenly she caught the first sounds of the motor and, as she spun around, the remarkably beautiful sight of the yacht at close quarters.

It was coming in fast, a rippling silver trail in its wake. There was a tall man at the helm, jet-black hair tossed into curls by the wind, his skin a very dark gold. She could only smile. He was spectacularly good looking. The answer to her dreams. Only he wasn't alone. Jane just had time to register an equally spectacular young woman standing near the rail when some swift-footed small creature went by her in a flash.

It was the aboriginal boy.

'Come back!' Jane shouted, petrified by the notion the boy was about to do something incredibly foolish, and just to oblige her he vaulted into the mooring-bay feet first and came up spouting water.

'Get out of there!' Jane ordered in sharp alarm,

struggling with her shoes because she knew any verbal effort wouldn't do the slightest bit of good. There were dozens of craft in the marina and visibility was cut by the density of hulls and masts and rigging. It was quite possible that the man on the yacht wouldn't see the boy until it was too late. She could feel the adrenalin pumping into her blood and she ran to the edge of the pontoon where the boy's head was bobbing and plunged in.

It was cold. Much colder than she expected, and while the pontoon rocked gently her skirt billowed like some improbable water lily, then collapsed like heavy seaweed against her chilled skin.

'Get out of here!' she begged the boy, flinging out a hand as he swam further away. 'Can't you see the danger?'

'No danger, Missy!' He stretched his neck above the water like some mythical sea-creature. 'You look silly!'

'You'll look silly minus an arm or a leg.' She struck out for him at the same time shouting, 'Help!' at the top of her lungs. Hundreds of dancing lights made a dazzle of the water, almost blinding her. 'Got you!' she cried determinedly and grabbed a slippery shoulder.

'Wotcha doin'?' The boy hit out at her crossly, obviously resenting her interference, but Jane gritted her teeth and somehow held on. Bag of bones though he might be, the boy was a wiry little devil.

'Ahoy there!' A man's dark, incisive voice rent the air, severe with shock and harsh rebuke. 'What the hell is going on?'

Jane lifted an arm and waved frantically. 'There's a child here. For God's sake, *stop!*' There was an awful ache in her other arm and for good measure the boy kicked her.

'It's me, Mister Mac!' he called joyously, then

flickered Jane a ferocious scowl. 'Why you afraid of trouble?'

'Because *you* must get in trouble all the time.' Intent as she was on holding the boy she heard the oath that ripped from the man's throat then the abrupt change in the motor as he selected reverse gear.

'Dive. Dive under the pier,' she ordered and got a strangle hold on the boy's skinny neck. It could be dangerous seconds before the reverse gear took hold.

She forced the boy into a dive and they went under the surface together. When they emerged on the other side, the yacht was standing off and the tall man was leaning over the side, an accelerated pulse in his dark temple betraying his fury.

'What kind of a lunatic game are you playing?'

Jane coughed up water, furious at the injustice. 'You tell me. Do I look like the boy's mother?'

'You risked getting your head split open or worse. Are you going to get out?'

'What the hell! I like a good soak.'

'Hiya, Mister Mac!' The aboriginal boy had lost none of his aplomb. He cocked his curly black head to one side and pointed to Jane. 'This sure one crazy lady.'

'And *you*'d know!' Jane had no hesitation in ducking him.

'Get out of there. *Both* of you,' the man ordered in a hard, clipped voice.

'Is it too much trouble for you to help us?' Jane called sweetly.

'I kun get outta here *myself*!' the boy told Jane with cheerful insolence and immediately demonstrated by lifting himself up on to the pontoon with his wiry arms. 'There, what did I tell ya!' he cried triumphantly.

Jane's legs were tired from treading water and she was hampered by the sodden weight of her full skirt.

'Next time I'll take good care to let you drown.'

'Not me, lady!' He motioned cockily with his head. 'Me swim like a fish.'

'So do I but I've no wish to die.'

The tall man interrupted by calling back something to his girl companion. Then in a kind of fulminating rage he cleared the distance between the yacht and the jetty and lifted Jane from the water as easily as he would have lifted some figurine from a table.

Despite herself Jane was enormously impressed. Slender as she was she nevertheless accounted for around one hundred and ten pounds.

'You're all right?' Brilliant blue eyes looked at her with both anger and admiration.

'You're too good to ask me.' Jane was tempted to sag against him but delicately held herself upright.

'I didn't hurt you, did I?' he asked with the faintest saving grace of anxiety.

'Not really.' She drew air back into her lungs, her darkened hair hanging like seagrape. 'What's an arm or two pulled out of its socket?'

'I certainly had no wish to hurt you. I simply had to get you out of there.'

'Thank you so much. I don't know what possessed me going to that dear little boy's rescue.' She bunched up folds of her skirt and tried to wring it out.

'Don't worry about that,' he told her curtly. 'We'll find you dry clothing. Obviously you haven't met Tulli before. He's a particularly worrying child, I'll grant you, but a lot smarter than you think.'

'*She* the silly one!' Tulli rocked on his bare heels. 'I wouldna got hurt, Missy.'

'So *you* say!' Jane countered. 'You can't continue to do this. It's dangerous.'

'Dangerous, what's that?' Tulli gave her another upward, insolent grin.

'It means you'll be barred from the marina if you ever do it again!' the tall man suddenly thundered. 'You know I can do it, and I will.'

'Sure, Mister Mac!' the boy's huge, black eyes almost lolled in his head. 'I jes' wanted to surprise you.'

'You've made me furious. You could have been injured only for the quick thinking of this very wet young woman. Are you going to thank her for your survival?'

'Thanks, Missy!' Tulli apologised to Jane obediently. He smiled too. 'You sure pretty!'

Oddly enough Jane's extreme wetness did make her look very seductive, her dress clinging to her like a second skin. 'Just don't do it again, Tulli,' she told him hurriedly, unable to control the faint flush that warmed her skin.

'You'd better come aboard,' the tall man told Jane briefly. 'You ought to dry off.' He took a step closer to her and Jane felt a peculiar weakness as though her legs were about to buckle beneath her. 'Please don't bother,' she went on quickly. 'I'm quite happy as I am.'

'Don't be ridiculous.' He half lifted a hand impatiently, then let it drop. It seemed he was almost as wary of touching her as she was wary of being touched by him.

'Can I come too, Mister Mac?' Tulli implored.

'No, you can't!' the tall man told him emphatically. 'You're lucky I don't paddle your backside.'

'Won't do it again, Mister Mac. Promise.' Tulli swallowed hugely.

'You're so damned right about that.' The tall man suddenly reached out and roughed up the boy's curls. 'Think about losing an arm or a leg. It would stop all your games.'

'She yell like anything!' Tulli responded in an instant, pantomiming Jane's waving and shouting.

'I'm sure I heard her. Lucky for *you*,' the boy's hero returned caustically. 'Cut along now, Tulli. I'm sure you have a good explanation why you're not in school.'

'Sick, Mister Mac,' the boy told him delightedly.

'And what about Melly?'

'She know I'm roaming.'

'I'll try to call in and speak to her tonight.'

'You'll *what*, Mister Mac?'

'You heard,' the tall man said hard-heartedly. 'Melly ought to be keeping an eye on you instead of looking for a husband.'

'She'll get one too!' Tulli smiled broadly, waved a hand and ran away.

'*Please*.' The boy's hero grasped Jane's arm authoritatively and assisted her on to the yacht. His female companion looked on sullenly like some sleek jungle feline flexing its muscles. Obviously the whole misadventure had earned her disapproval and there were impatient frown lines between her black brows.

'My cousin, Antonella.' The man introduced her briefly. 'Alex McGovern, at your service.'

Jane still possessed sufficient wit to remain calm. As ye sow, so shall ye reap! Even Cousin Antonella's smouldering hostility had its place in this strange circumstance.

'Sandro is never one to turn away a lady in distress,' Antonella now announced in a lush, accented mezzo clanging with sarcasm. Every time she breathed her golden breasts heaved, barely contained in a black bikini-top which she wore with very short black and white patterned shorts. She exuded sexuality in a way Jane had seldom come across, but then, so did *he*. They were the most riveting, physically stunning pair she had ever seen.

'If I could just borrow a caftan, wrap-around, anything,' Jane suggested. 'I'm Jane Gilmour, by the way.'

'You're a visitor?' His handsome, dangerous face was illuminated by a faint smile, like a sunburst in a stormy sky.

'Only just arrived.' Jane grasped her hair and pulled it together at the nape of her neck.

'I suppose I *could* lend you a caftan.' The girl, Antonella, moved swiftly, breaking her cousin's blue gaze. She indicated to Jane to follow her below. 'Our figures are not at all the same but it should do quite well.'

'You're very kind,' Jane murmured politely, not much liking being in the position where she had to accept anything. 'I'm staying at the Hibiscus Lodge. I'll get it back to you as soon as possible.

'I should hope so!' Antonella shook back her curling hair. 'It is very expensive. My clothes are all from Italy.'

In a small forward cabin Jane stripped off her wet garments and towelled herself hastily, keeping the lemon towel around her while she blow-dried her hair. Antonella's manner had said it all. Get dressed and get going. Perhaps she would have been treated better had she been much older or alternatively awfully plain.

The caftan wasn't much like an ordinary garment. It was brilliantly coloured in a striking, original design and the material was of the finest. Jane slipped it over her head, reacting to its silky sensuous feel against her all but naked body. Ankle-length on her, for she was some inches taller than the petite Antonella, but slighter and narrower everywhere else. Her breasts were high and cone-shaped whereas Antonella's were round and full. Her hair that had grown just below shoulder length now fell in a thick, straight ash-gold mass and probably the brilliant colours of the caftan made her green eyes bigger and bolder. They were certainly arresting in her creamy-pale face. Antonella had given her a coral-coloured plastic carry-bag from an island resort and Jane pushed her wet folded clothes into it, reflecting her shoes were out there somewhere on the jetty. At least it wouldn't be necessary to shuffle back to the Lodge bare footed.

When she found her way back to the saloon, Alex McGovern was pouring steaming black coffee.

'Milk, cream?' He only glanced at her but Jane had the unnerving feeling she was completely naked.

'Black would be fine. You really shouldn't have bothered.'

'No bother at all, I assure you.' He had very elegant, long-fingered hands, now he gestured her towards the semicircular banquette that served the dining-table. 'My apologies if I sounded somewhat harsh. You gave me a rather bad shock.'

For the first time Jane allowed him a smile and he looked at her long and very searchingly. 'I must apologise also,' Jane said. 'I was a little short myself. I really didn't think you'd see us in time and the little wretch kicked me.'

'He *hurt* you?' Those blue eyes continued to study her.

'Not really!' Jane shrugged and slid into the leather-upholstered banquette. 'Looking at him one wouldn't know the secret of his strength.'

'You had to be crazy doing such a thing!' Antonella announced scornfully. 'That little brat knows well what he's doing.'

'Maybe he does, but I couldn't take the chance.'

Alex McGovern moved lithely towards the table, setting Jane's coffee before her. 'You took a considerable risk,' he said gravely, 'but be assured that little monkey won't try the same thing again. We all spoil him. Both his parents were killed in a cyclone and a young sister is all he has left. She's a sweet, silly little thing. Little more than a child herself. I'll have to arrange something.'

'*Please*, Sandro, don't you do enough?' Antonella angled her small, luscious body into the banquette. 'Are you a tourist?' she demanded suddenly of Jane.

'No, here on business.' Jane shook her head.

'Are you going to tell us what?'

Up close Antonella was remarkably like the young Lollobrigida in type but without the underlying humour that characterised La Lollo's gorgeous face.

'It's all very hush-hush at the moment,' Jane explained apologetically. Liz wouldn't applaud her for pre-empting her position and authority.

'Maybe you're spying out the land for an 'otel?' Antonella suggested, looking across at Jane in a challenging way. 'If so, you are wasting your time. Tell her, Sandro!' R's rolled off her tongue in the most seductive way.

'Not a hotel,' Jane said in what she hoped was a convincing tone.

To her surprise Alex McGovern sat down beside her. 'Than what is your story, Miss Gilmour? I feel sure you've got one.'

Jane merely shrugged in a calm way. 'I assure you I'm not here as a McGovern competitor. It's simply that I'm not at liberty to say at this time. I'm only an employee.'

'The boss's secretary?' Antonella laughed suggestively.

'Actually, yes.' Jane's sea-green eyes were limpid. 'Secretary, assistant, girl-Friday. My boss is a woman.'

'Would you care for something with that?' Alex

McGovern asked her. 'I'm quite forgetting my manners.'

'No, thank you. The coffee's fine.' Indeed it was very good.

'You say you've just arrived?' The startlingly blue eyes moved over her with a considerable degree of speculation.

'Hmmm. This afternoon. I love the sea, boats, so I came across to have a closer look at the marina.'

'Then your time isn't so valuable,' Antonella purred. 'How long do you intend to stay in the north?'

'That's not at all clear,' Jane answered mildly. 'It might only be the matter of a day.'

'Antonella.' Alex McGovern gave his cousin a quelling smile. 'We don't usually interrogate our guests.'

'Only when they fall in on us,' Antonella responded, and a flush darkened her deep golden skin. 'Miss Gilmour might well represent some entrepreneur trying to cut in on McGovern territory.'

'You own this part of the world?' Jane asked innocently.

Antonella looked outraged but Alex McGovern only lifted one black eyebrow looking faintly amused. 'Pretty well, Miss Gilmour. I'm sure you're every bit as innocent as you look. Already you've performed an heroic act. One unthinking small boy might have been seriously injured but for you. Perhaps you and your employer would care to have dinner with us one evening? A small gesture of gratitude.'

'*Sandro!*' Antonella's huge, black eyes flashed, but somehow he failed to take the hint.

'Tomorrow night? Do you think that would suit? I would send a car to your hotel. Monteverdi—my home—is some distance away.'

He was watching her closely. Too closely, Jane

thought. His superb, dark-golden tanned skin threw his eyes into dazzling relief.

'Why I'm sure my employer would be delighted!' she said with perfect truth. 'I've been told about northern hospitality.'

'It's clear we can't let you go without saying thank you,' he returned suavely. 'If I didn't, I'm sure it would return to haunt me.'

'Could we go into town, Sandro?' Antonella flashed him a loaded glance. 'I have a few things to do.'

'Certainly, *cara*.' He withdrew his gaze from the pure outline of Jane's profile. 'We'll escort Miss Gilmour back to her hotel.'

Liz when she heard was ecstatic. 'I can't believe this!' She put her arms across her breast and hugged herself. 'You're sure you're not putting me on?'

'It happened just as I said.' Jane had sent Antonella's caftan off to be carefully dry-cleaned and now she sat in Liz's room wrapped in her pretty floral robe.

'You step out for a walk and you meet Alex McGovern?'

'I'm sure if we'd planned it it couldn't have gone better.'

'But the coincidence, my dear! Perhaps it's *fate!*'

Jane sat back so that her face was in shadow. 'I think we'd better tell him before we go.'

'I'd certainly like to,' Liz agreed smartly. 'The thing is he could refuse to see us if we sprang it on him just like that. We've already learnt they're infernally touchy.'

'He's not a man I'd care to cross,' Jane said very fervently, 'and the cousin seems to have some kind of manic obsession about protecting him and the family interests. In fact, only she's his cousin, or so he claimed, I'd say she was madly in love with him.'

'Cousins get married all the time.'

'Okay—well it's difficult, Liz.' Jane didn't want to think about Alex McGovern marrying his cousin and switched off.

'You think he'll agree to see us if we spring it on him now? He could, as you say, think it all a ploy.'

'It would have been very difficult to arrange the timing.'

'Two-bit opportunists make the time,' Liz pointed out. 'My intention was to ring him and arrange an appointment. Now I think we'd better keep our identity under wraps. At least until after dinner.'

'How long do you think it would be before the questions started?' Jane countered. 'They'll throw everything at you.'

'I suppose.' Liz stroked her cheek, a mannerism of hers when she was dealing with something unforeseen. 'I'll just ring him up in the morning and tell him the facts. I expect he'll cancel the dinner.'

'I detest doing things under false pretences. Anyway, you're a distinguished film-producer. Let him think about that!'

'I'm thinking more about being hit by a law-suit. The very last thing I want is to offend these people. It's a devilish tickly situation . . .'

'Play straight with him, Liz,' Jane warned.

'Well, he certainly made an impression on you,' Liz said almost challengingly. 'You'd think he was a bloody Pharaoh.'

'I suspect he lives like one,' Jane returned simply. 'I don't feel good about this, Liz. I'm getting bad vibes. That Antonella is a funny girl. Very passionate and temperamental. She really comes on.'

'And McGovern?' Liz stared down into Jane's

worried face.

'As smooth as they come and he absolutely reeks power. There's no doubting his Mediterranean heritage. He's staggeringly handsome. In fact I've never seen a more handsome man on or off film. He has very darkly tanned olive skin, raven-black hair with a decided curl, the sort of bones Michelangelo sculpted in his best form, but he's not sort of shortish and compact like a lot of Italians, he's very tall, about six three, ultra lean, and his eyes are an unbelievable deep ocean blue. He's a mixture of races and it all adds up to something terribly turbulent and exotic. I guess what I'm trying to say is he's a proud, high-mettled man. Trying to put something over him could turn out to be a terrible disaster.'

'I think you've made your point, dear,' Liz said mildly. 'Such a coup your meeting him like that yet it's turned into a complication. Of course I'll ring him in the morning. I can't think he *will* take back that invitation.'

As it would happen, both of them slept in and when Liz got through to the Monteverdi residence some short time after breakfast, she was informed that Mr McGovern could not be contacted for the rest of the day.

'Flown off to some island or other,' she explained. 'Didn't Jean at reception tell us they're developing a resort?'

'Hmmm, Mandeville, Mandevilla, I'm not sure. It's supposed to have an extensive fringing reef. One of the continental islands, I believe. We'll have to ask some more.'

'So what do we do now?' Liz stepped out on to the flower-lined balcony. 'I couldn't leave a message and I wouldn't care to ring him half an hour before we arrive.'

'We should have rung him last night,' Jane reasoned belatedly. 'It's going to be terribly awkward.'

She still thought so sitting in the back of a chauffeur-driven Rolls-Royce that same evening. The driver was keeping a frequent eye on them but after the initial exchanges had lapsed into a resolved silence.

'Probably doesn't speak English very well,' Liz hissed in Jane's ear, earning another basilisk glance in the rear-vision mirror.

'Don't count on it,' Jane murmured and stared out of the window. It was true their driver had a very thick accent but Jane was quite sure he understood English perfectly. She even had the funny notion he was keeping an eye on them as though he thought they could well turn out to be industrial spies.

Jane, glancing sideways at the very smartly dressed Liz, in a Chanel-style evening suit in black and gold, thought that for once in her life Liz was looking less than sure of herself. Liz had in fact tried to contact Alex McGovern again late afternoon only to be cut off rather abruptly by a female voice telling her Mr McGovern was very busy and could not come to the phone.

'She sounded insufferably arrogant,' Liz had complained.

'Well you certainly tried! It was probably Cousin Antonella.' Jane was sure of it. 'She was extraordinarily put out when he issued the invitation. Mere mortals apparently don't rate an entrée.'

'I think I'll explain myself *after* not *before* dinner,' Liz said.

Now she stared at Jane's intent profile and reached out and patted Jane's hand. 'Everything's going to be all right,' she murmured reassuringly. 'Anyway, you look marvellous. Like an Easter lily.'

Jane had certainly tried. In fact they had both worked on looking good. Jane wore white, a simple camisole bodice with a full skirt made into something exceptional by the use of the finest semi-sheer cotton with lace inserts. It was a very pretty, summery dress, soft and feminine, and because there were exquisite gardenias blooming profusely on their balcony she had fixed one perfect flower to hold back the left side of her hair and brushed the other into a shining, swinging curtain with the ends curving under. She hoped Alex McGovern would be pleasantly surprised. She didn't consider she had been seen at her best.

The drive was longer than either of them expected, a good half-hour, the last ten minutes between great stretches of cane that rose like the great pillars of a temple. Cane without a break.

'God, I'm beginning to feel claustrophobic,' Liz laughingly moaned. 'I suppose it's alive with snakes and toads. Want to get out and see?'

'I'd be petrified with fright.' Looking through the window Jane could see they were coming a lot closer to an incredible monolith of a mountain that rose sheer from the luxuriant jungle and dominated the town. It jutted up like a great jagged finger with a hump, black against the majestic sky, and Jane realised it sat directly at Monteverdi's back door. The plantation house and its outfields occupied most of the coastal shelf looking out on the gloriously coloured bay. By day the mountain, like all the tropical vegetation, would be a lush, brilliant green which would account for the plantation name. Monteverdi—Green Mountain.

There was nothing really to tell them they were on the estate until the road divided into a great circular drive enclosing a private rain-forest. The driver switched to main beam and a great Curtain Fig tree sprang up before them, its huge aerial roots all but strangling the host.

'Looks like we're here!' Liz whispered, her strong mobile features highly expressive. 'It all looks terribly grand.'

Even then the house was a shock.

It stood up on a high knoll with glorious views in all directions. The mountain rose up behind it like the jagged misty mountains in Japanese watercolours, great shade trees framed it on either side and running away down a series of spectacular watergardens that were cleverly lit at night was a parkland that stopped a scant thirty feet from the huge shining crescent of white sand.

'Will you look at that!' Liz muttered urgently. 'It ought to be in Italy!'

'Extraordinary!' Jane agreed, and gave Liz a warning poke in case she forgot and started talking about exploiting it as a location.

'However did they build such a place in the jungle?' Liz nudged her back. 'How did they get the craftsmen? Let alone here. It would have been virtual jungle.'

Cheap labour, Jane thought but never said aloud. For her part she had been profoundly disturbed by the plantation's history. She thought of the tragic Contessa. Beautiful as this tropical environment was, it must have seemed a God-forsaken wilderness to an Italian aristocrat in a hemisphere not her own. In those early days the frontier north would have been raw and violent. Even if the Contessa had worshipped her husband, Jane could easily understand how much an alien and relatively primitive world could have caused her to go into a deep and lasting depression. The old story of the 'Sugar King' wasn't just dramatic, it was tragic.

'Let me do all the talking,' Liz told Jane quietly. 'I defy anyone to resist my persuasive powers!'

'Do I detect just the faintest tremor?'

'You do.'

The chauffeur assisted them to alight, then they were walking up a broad flight of stone steps that led to a magnificent portico protecting the marble-floored entrance hall.

''Struth!' Liz muttered irreverently. 'Wouldn't it be sensible to put in a lift?'

'Our host is nowhere in sight,' Jane managed with bright courage.

'Yes, he is, dear.' Liz's commanding voice was curiously excited. 'Very tall and lean? He's coming through the door. You really think I look all right?'

'You look terrific, Liz,' Jane wasn't flattering her boss, it was true. Dressed up as she was tonight, Liz Stoddart cut a striking figure.

'Ah, Miss Stoddart, Miss Gilmour!' Alex McGovern came down to meet them. He had a compellingly attractive voice. A heartbreaking kind of voice, Jane thought, dark and resonant but with a thread of steel. It was the sort of voice that was capable of every nuance. Now it sounded suave, good-humoured, charmingly self-assured.

'Mr McGovern, I know it is!' Liz responded with equal aplomb, holding out her hand. 'How very kind of you to invite us to your marvellous home.'

'My pleasure.' His racial mixture showed in a very European bow. 'It's just such a pity you were not able to contact me today. You *did* ring?'

'I did.' Liz, expecting a handsome man, thought 'handsome' didn't say it at all. Alex McGovern was dynamite.

'But you're here!' He turned to Jane commenting on the gardenia she wore in her hair. 'I don't think anything complements a woman's beauty more than a flower.'

'Garbo thought that when she was on the screen,' Liz laughed, obviously thinking she could surmount any obstacle with a sense of humour. 'This is my first trip to this part of the world. Jane and I have been revelling in its exotica.'

'Yet my image was you were here for work no matter what.' He halted Jane with a hand on her arm. A shoot of a remarkable orange-coloured bougainvillaea that grew in a great rampart over a series of white columns threatened to snag her skirt and he held it away.

'Thank you.' She knew her voice shook a little. She quivered when he touched her, when a man's touch on her arm was commonplace. 'We allowed ourselves the day to adjust to the climate.'

'I thought you had adjusted remarkably well by yesterday afternoon.'

It was said very smoothly, almost admiringly, yet Jane immediately threw up a defensive barrier. He was too much of the tycoon not to have had them checked out right down to their dental records. Yet he confounded her by courteously taking Liz's arm and responding charmingly to her series of questions about the architecture of the house.

'You sound like a writer, Miss Stoddart,' he said with a devastatingly interested expression. 'Are you?'

Liz gave a half-explosive, half-wary laugh. 'I did write the script for a film once.'

'Fascinating!' He paused to look down into Liz's uplifted face. 'From a novel or did you make it up?'

'A bit of both, I guess!' Liz admitted with amused pride. 'Do you know anything of my work, Mr McGovern?'

'Alas, *no*, but I expect to change all that.'

'I think you're testing me.' Liz sounded as though the challenge pleased her.

'Hardly that, Miss Stoddart. You are my guest.' Tall as Liz was she had to tilt her head to look up at him. 'Utterly everything is coloured by that.'

As for Jane! She didn't think they could rely on the pleasantness to last. Obviously Alex McGovern was playing the game on his terms.

Visions of elegance and beauty and grandeur intruded on them almost immediately as they moved through the huge entrance hall past the main reception rooms towards the core of the house.

'The family are waiting for us in the atrium,' he told them. 'You'll want a drink before dinner.'

The atrium turned out to be an incredibly spectacular room with a glass ceiling and a tiled floor. The ceiling was supported by slender barley-twist columns capped by a series of archways. There were lush, tropical plants blooming everywhere in beautiful ceramic planters or suspended from the ceiling and the most glorious assemblage of orchids Jane had ever seen. They were breathtaking in their beauty and she looked in, enchanted.

'After dinner I'll take you around and let you memorise all the names.' For an instant Alex McGovern regarded her soft expression.

'I'd like that.' She knew she sounded faintly breathless, but frankly she found him extravagantly unnerving. Jane liked men. She enjoyed their company. She adored her father and she had been reared with the best of brothers yet she didn't define herself in terms of men. She considered herself man's equal, but now for the first time she was coming under the domination of a sophisticated man's aura. His sexual aura she had to admit. His face, his voice, seemed to be inhabited by a tremendous awareness, ever-changing responses that gave the sculptured features such devastating life, the voice the dark delight.

'What a wonderful room!' Liz, too, was bewitched. She reached out and touched Alex McGovern's jacketed arm. 'I've been infatuated with Italian design since my early days. The Grand Tour, you know!'

As they approached, a distinguished-looking man in his early fifties stood up; obviously a relative because he shared a certain familial resemblance with Alex McGovern without the Mediterranean cast. He looked more the craggy Scot. A sweet-faced middle-aged woman gave them a smile at one point and Antonella, resplendent in brilliant yellow, swung a small gold-sandalled foot in a manner that suggested she might like to kick someone.

Alex McGovern made the introductions with practised ease. From left to right, his uncle Robert, the handsomeness reduced by a beaky nose, Robert's wife, Helen, and of course the tempestuous Antonella who looked like she was just waiting for the moment to work off her feelings.

'My grandmother retires early these days,' Alex McGovern explained. 'She is the McGovern matriarch and rigorous upholder of the family traditions.'

They all sat down in white, Indian-cotton-upholstered rattan chairs and shortly after a Chinese manservant in black trousers and a white jacket brought them the pre-dinner drink they had ordered, then moved off quietly.

'Alex tells us you saved that little scamp, Tulli, from possible injury, Miss Gilmour?' Helen McGovern smiled. 'It was too bad you had to take such an unexpected dip.'

'He did give me a fright,' Jane admitted. 'I'd been watching him clowning for ten minutes or more but I never expected for a moment he would dive in the mooring-bay. I really don't think he saw the danger.'

'Well then, to your quick thinking!' Alex McGovern raised his glass and the others followed suit.

Liz then took off on a similar funny experience which was to set the mood for the best part of dinner. The conversation ranged over a wide variety of subjects, substantially pleasant, their laughter mingled, but Jane had the unsettling notion the family had decided in advance to allow their guests to enjoy the meal before introducing more provocative topics.

They were sitting enjoying coffee and liqueurs in the magnificent Grand Salon before the conversation took the abrupt turn Jane had been dreading.

'The message, of course, you were trying to get to me this morning was, you are in your professional life, Miss Stoddart, a film-producer?'

There was dignity in the quick turn of Liz's head. 'There was no deception whatever intended.' Liz caught Helen McGovern's troubled eyes and smiled at her. 'Jane and I were both anxious to let you know the reason for our being here before enjoying your wonderful hospitality but there simply wasn't the opportunity. I rang again this afternoon.'

'What time?'

'It would have been five-ish,' Liz said.

'You were here.' Helen McGovern glanced at Alex who placed his coffee-cup down on the table.

'I never heard of it.'

'But surely,' Liz looked faintly aghast, 'I spoke to a young woman'—she took good care not to look at Antonella—'and I was told Mr McGovern was too busy to come to the phone.'

'It might be worth while to check that out, Helen,' Alex McGovern advised in a dispassionate kind of voice. 'Any member of the staff would know to check with me before making excuses.'

'I was with Miss Stoddart at the time,' Jane volunteered, underscoring Liz's trustworthiness.

'Of course, Miss Gilmour.' Alex McGovern gave her another one of his electric-blue glances. 'I wasn't trying to lead you into a trap.'

'Neither did we wish to come here with any-thing——'

'Devious?'

'*Unspoken* between us.'

'Very commendable,' he said coolly, apparently untouched by her earnestness. 'Nevertheless you have been dreading this moment.'

'We've been looking forward to it!' Liz interrupted vigorously. 'We've had a most enjoyable evening and it's possible, if you agree,' she looked around the rest of the family, 'we could have a worth-while discussion about my current project. I am a film-producer as you've obviously found out and I've come here with the express purpose of enlisting your invaluable support and co-operation.'

'Miss Gilmour would have taken a header into the bay regardless.'

'Certainly when I see a child about to perish.' Jane's luminous green eyes began to sparkle. 'I realise it was quite extraordinary meeting you that way.'

'You connived at it, I think.' Antonella who had been smouldering quietly cast Jane a contemptuous glance.

'Absolutely *not*!'

Alex McGovern's smile was cynical. 'We believe you, Miss Gilmour. Though you'll have to agree people in your line of work seldom let opportunities pass them by.'

'I wouldn't have known you from Adam,' she pointed out.

'Adam wasn't very well known in these parts.' His blue eyes raked over her.

'Alex, darling.' Helen looked as though she thought the exchange had gone far enough. 'I can't think Jane is enjoying this situation.'

'She didn't back away from it either.'

'I expect she has to do what she's told,' Helen said vaguely. Not knowing quite what to expect at the outset, Helen was relieved to find her worst fears abated. Liz Stoddart, though a tireless striver after her own ends, was unquestionably highly intelligent and even kind and Helen had taken an enormous liking to her young assistant. Now she sought to protect her from the family wrath, forgetting her own initial reactions of dismay when Alex had presented them with a mini-dossier on Liz Stoddart Productions.

'Shall we come to the point then, Miss Stoddart?' Alex was suggesting now. 'You intend to film Armstrong's novel?'

Liz leaned forward and pressed her hands together. 'When you read the script, Mr McGovern, you'll realise it will make a very beautiful and exciting film. I'm against doing anything people don't want, which is why I think we should have this talk.'

'Why on earth?' he asked suavely. 'I understand the script is already in its final form and the players selected. No doubt Miss Gilmour here is to play the governess, Laura Hamilton. The English flower who bloomed into a shameless temptress.'

Liz was so jolted her mouth fell open. 'My dear Mr McGovern, Jane is not an actress.'

'An actress any time she cares to be,' he contradicted flatly. 'As I see it, there are two courses of action. One, we make it as difficult as possible for you to proceed and I think you should be warned most people prefer not to fight us, or two, you re-write your script to our satisfaction.'

'Please, won't you read the present version first? It's beautiful, powerful!'

'Why not?' he shrugged eloquently. 'You have everything to make it a great box-office success. Colonial days at their most violent, passions running high, hatred, bitterness, dementia, murder. Audiences don't trouble to differentiate between fiction and fact. Armstrong's book is the worst possible mix of both. He took a real-life character, my ancestor as it happened, the circumstances of his life, the triumphs and tragedies, and dressed it up as a work of fiction. My family have never escaped notoriety because of that book. Ugly rumours are easily spawned, especially against the rich and powerful. I have never understood how Armstrong escaped retribution.'

Looking at his face, Jane shivered. 'We're playing it as a total work of fiction. We understand your fears, Mr McGovern.'

'You do not!' He looked at the shining bell of her hair and her creamy, oval face. 'Your over-riding interest is a box-office success. Who cares if it opens up old wounds?'

'But surely, Mr McGovern,' Liz said with a trace of distress, 'very few people could possibly know it's based on a real-life character?'

The vibrant voice went cold. 'Just about everyone will after your publicity people peddle it to the media. John McGovern was a great man, a great pioneer. He did not found this country's sugar industry though a fellow Scot did, but in his day he enjoyed equivalent status. He was the greatest plantation owner of the north. He became enormously wealthy it is true through the gold of the harvest and the gold from the mines but this country benefited and so did its people.

He was not a man to do away with his wife so he could take a mistress, governess to his children. From every account he would have been well able to manage both. He wasn't a gentle man—he was one of the toughest men of his day—but he was a man of honour. We will not see that honour defiled.'

Such power was in his face, such fire, Jane felt her mouth go dry. Beneath the veneer of smooth sophistication he was like some dark and dangerous animal.

'Please, won't you read the script, Mr McGovern?' she begged him. 'It makes no judgments. It presents a series of events, the entanglement of lives. This was a vast new country, largely unknown. The question of what happened to *Andrew Ogilvie's* Contessa, important though it is, is not the big thing of the film. It's a saga of one man's fight in the land of opportunity. It encompasses so many aspects of colonial life—the titanic struggles against nature, the colour-problems peculiar to the north, the way Dr Lang virtually harangued the British Government into sending settlers to the tropical north. He knew white men could and would grow cotton, sugar, tobacco. He influenced men like Louis Hope and John McGovern. The settlers came and because they came a new nation rose to greatness. That's what our film is all about. Liquid gold and gold from one of the world's greatest mines. Andrew Ogilvie *is* a hero.'

'And the screenplay, where is it?'

'Why it's back at the Lodge.' Jane glanced at Liz who was looking enormously fascinated.

'Mightn't we read it, Alex?' Robert McGovern appealed to his nephew for the first time. Senior though he was in terms of years there was no doubting who had the real power. 'Did any of us ever think we'd be left in peace? The private lives of prominent people seem to be public property. Even the Queen of England has had her privacy violated. We can fight you, Miss Stoddart. Force you to go elsewhere. This is *still* McGovern country, but in the end you'll make your film.'

'Nonna, what about Nonna?' Antonella's jet-black eyes flashed. 'Who could be so cruel to her? She is so old, so fragile. She remembers the wicked rumours that persisted for so many years.'

'Won't you please read the screenplay?' Liz persisted quietly. 'All of you. I promise you it's beautiful, spellbinding.'

'And the disappearance of the Contessa?' Alex McGovern asked harshly.

Liz hesitated, sinking her strong white teeth on her bottom lip. 'The audience are allowed to make their own judgment on that.'

'Really?' he smiled grimly, one black eyebrow lifting. 'We have water lilies up here that spread creamy petals from a golden heart and they're deadly. Your governess? I'm sure you have made her an innocent.'

For some reason Jane reacted as though the slight had been cast at her. Her beautiful skin suffused with colour, pomegranate against the cream. 'Why should she be victimised because she cared terribly?' she charged him emotionally. 'She is presented as an innocent. An innocent in a violent Eden. It would be marvellous if we could all love to order, but we can't. It isn't even a question of wanting, things happen. Passion interferes in countless lives. It brings out the best and worst in people. Laura Hamilton didn't come to a new country because she wanted to. She had to accept what employment she could. She didn't want to fall in love with her employer—a married man. Nor he with her. It just happened with no one to blame.'

'You know all this. You were there?' His handsome face was both amused and contemptuous.

'It's what our film will tell happened.'

His brilliant eyes studied her ironically. 'You would be most moving as Laura. Obviously you identify with her.'

'One of our leading young actresses has already been assigned the part,' Liz told him in a surprised tone. 'Jane has no experience whatever.'

'Neither has many a discovery,' he pointed out with easy insolence. 'The only way this family will consider your aims and your needs is to have final say on the script. That done, we will make the estate available and house your main people. The rest can be accommodated in the town. Rewrite the script to our satisfaction and this family will be willing to come in as an investor. If you don't agree we can stop you from making your film in this part of the world. You'll need food, lodging, supplies, an efficient communications system. In short, lots of help. McGovern interests cover a good deal of territory and we have a good deal of influence naturally. One must applaud the excellence of our young industry, and your part in it Miss Stoddart, but I know for a fact you don't work on big budgets. Satisfy us with your screenplay and you will get our co-operation. Otherwise ...' He paused eloquently for all the world more like some ruthless Renaissance prince than a New-world tycoon.

Liz's misgivings were all too apparent in her expression. 'We couldn't interfere with the characters too much, Mr McGovern. The love triangle is terribly important but I assure you the dialogue is most moving, most subtle. Bryan Rowland is responsible. You remember he created a sensation when his first novel appeared.'

'I notice he hasn't contrived to come up with another.'

'He's a marvellous writer,' Jane said. 'I'm sure when you have the opportunity to study the screenplay you'll admire his work.'

'Get him here,' Alex McGovern ordered abruptly. 'I am certain we will make changes.'

'I would have to confer with my colleagues first,' Liz told him a shade haggardly. 'Perry Wyndham has returned from America to direct. I'm sure he will want to know the results of our conversation.'

'Certainly,' Alex McGovern agreed suavely. 'It will hasten our negotiations if I see the screenplay as soon as possible. I'm sure you won't mind leaving Miss Gilmour here, when you fly off.'

CHAPTER THREE

THE following morning Jane tapped on the connecting door gently. 'Liz, are you awake?'

'No, dear, I'm a poor tormented soul wandering through purgatory,' Liz responded.

That could only mean one thing. Liz had one of her migraines.

'Why didn't you tell me?' Jane found her way gropingly across the darkened room. 'Have you lost your vision?'

'A big weal on one eye. Just like a horror movie.'

'Oh, how frightful! Have you had your medication?'

'Yes, dear, what is that that just fell over?'

'Your suitcase. You left it in the middle of the floor. Of course you know what set it off.'

'The suitcase?'

'The migraine. What an impossibly arrogant man he is. He's going much too far if he thinks I'm going to stay as some kind of hostage.'

'You might have to, dear girl. Oh, God,' Liz winced and was forced to lie back. 'He really is a hero-villain. The only way we can possibly succeed is get him on-side. I didn't enjoy upsetting Helen McGovern and the uncle. They sure covered their feelings for most of the evening but I guessed all along they were on to us.'

'Obviously if you have money, connections, you can check anyone out. He probably runs his own private Mafia.'

'We can't fight him.' Liz pressed clammy fingers beside her eyes as though willing the pain to go away. 'I wouldn't dare. As far as that goes he could play our main character. A McGovern playing himself. That cousin of his made me uncomfortable, smouldering on the couch. What's it to her? She doesn't even live here.'

'You won't believe this but she's a member of the Raffaelli family, a descendent of McGovern's Contessa.'

'For heaven's sake!' Liz was so surprised she lifted her head. 'Who told you that?'

'Helen McGovern. I remember feeling . . . shocked.'

'Well that explains it,' Liz moaned. 'We don't go in for that vengeance, vendetta stuff, but in a lot of ways Alex McGovern himself acts impossibly medieval. I guess they still live a pretty feudal sort of life. I won't be able to get that script to him today. Have you thought of that?'

'It's so important I'd better do it,' Jane said, picking up Liz's long silk scarf and folding it. 'Perry is going to hate the idea of changing anything, let alone Bryan.'

'Bryan does what he's told,' Liz reminded her, matter-of-fact. 'You weren't imagining that cousin is in love with him. She *burns* for him. You only have to look at her.'

'I'd rather not,' Jane said wryly. 'Glances from her are like so many thrown daggers. Did you notice how hostile she is to me?'

'Because he finds you attractive,' Liz said, taking a deep, painful breath.

'Oh, no,' Jane shook her head. 'He's definitely not attracted to me. The initial charm is only a veneer. He reminds me of a stalking panther.'

'I won't argue with you, dear,' Liz said. 'So you're antagonistic to each other? That doesn't mean you wouldn't have been attracted under different circumstances. I'd better send you out there if you want to go. Reception can arrange transportation. Or would

you prefer to wait for me? With any luck I'll be over
the worst of it tomorrow.'

Jane, who had been sitting on a chair, stood up, her
eyes moving over Liz's prone figure. 'I think the best
thing to do is deliver it this morning. It will save a
day.'

'Well, I have taught you everything I know.'

'Could you possibly eat breakfast?'

'No.' Liz's strong body twitched. 'Breakfast would
be impossible though you might get them to send up a
pot of tea.'

'Anything else?' Jane moved over and touched Liz's
shoulder.

'Yes, dear.' Liz's expressive dark eyes were earnest.
'Take care.'

Jean at reception arranged a car, a little Japanese
runabout, and an hour later Jane was out on the open
road heading towards Monteverdi. It was a glorious
day—a cloudless peacock-blue sky, rippling cane,
gaudy parrots diving into the great mango trees and
dominating the distant skyline the strange, jagged
shape of Monteverdi. Helen McGovern had told her
an early explorer had called it Mount Garnet but John
McGovern had renamed it Monteverdi and the name
had stuck. It was a sombre-looking mountain in many
respects, dense with rain-forest and impossible to
climb beyond the hump. Great pythons lived in the
rain-forest, killing by strangling their prey within their
coils. The distinctive appearance of the rain-forest
fascinated her. Despite the hazards she would dearly
love to explore some part of it with a guide.

Alex McGovern?

Even the thought of him made her give a convulsive
swallow. She had never in her life met a human being
to take her breath away but her sensitivity to his aura

was so piercing it cut her to the quick. Even her skin prickled and tingled like an unwanted involuntary thrill. There *were* men to make a woman seethe and smoulder, look at Antonella, but Jane wasn't finding the sensations gratifying. She liked to feel in control of her life.

The little car was belting along peacefully when out of the blue it began to cough and shudder.

'Oh, no!' Jane took her eyes from the road and anxiously skimmed the dash. The temperature gauge was normal, the petrol gauge registered slightly over a quarter of a tank. Other than that what was wrong with it was right out of her ken. The car staggered on for another twenty feet and Jane steered it off to the narrow, grassy verge. It looked very much like she would have to continue the journey on foot. She hadn't encountered a soul on the road and in any case she had made the turn-off to Monteverdi. She estimated she had a good fifteen minutes' walk to be even inside the plantation-house compound. If the petrol gauge hadn't registered a quarter she could have sworn she was out of petrol but then again the gauge could be reading wrong.

A walk didn't bother her. Normally she enjoyed it but those high walls of cane made her just the least little bit nervous. It was just like walking a narrow path through a jungle and she would have to keep an eye out that no sun-basking snake blocked her path. Taipans she knew were dark brown with pale yellow undersides. Their venom was only slightly less powerful than that of the Tiger Snake, the most dangerous snake known. The tropical warmth that brought out the brilliant birds and stimulated the millions of flowers also roused the reptiles.

Jane locked the car from a long-established habit and took to the road. Nothing bothered her. Birds dived over the cane and there were countless rustlings in the giant grass but she saw no other form of life.

By the time she reached the great circular drive the heat had absorbed most of her energy. This was her first experience of the tropics and she saw now why people moved so much more slowly. She was wearing a shoulder-knotted loose cotton top over a matching pale-apricot gathered skirt and she was glad now of its cool design. The heavy hair that swung on her nape was damp with sweat and the cool air and the massive shade from the great shade trees enveloped her like a benediction.

The frond of a magnificent fern some fifteen feet long obscured a sign and as Jane ventured closer to read it she found it constituted a powerful warning. Guard dogs patrolled the estate and even as she froze rigid, out of the corner of her eye she detected movement in the golden-green gloom of the forest.

She spun quickly and the hairs stood up on the nape of her neck. A powerful Dobermann was nosing through the thick carpet of fallen leaves on the ground and immediately behind it another Dobermann stood immobile, fully alert, its ears pricked, its powerful sleek body poised to lunge forward. Its large wide mouth was open and its tongue lolled as it registered the far-away movements of a potential prey.

'Help!' Jane looked around frantically for the right tree to climb. A monster with fourteen-feet-high buttresses presented itself like a miracle. If she could climb it, could the dogs? They could certainly run up the ledge of great prop roots but she could use those thick woody vines to pull herself higher and higher.

All action came together. The dogs lunged and Jane propelled herself up the rain-forest giant with fantastic speed. These weren't the sort of dogs she was used to. These dogs were killers. Their frantic barking carried powerfully in the morning air, ear-splitting at close quarters as the canopy of the forest held in the sound like some great auditorium. They climbed higher up the woody ledge, one tumbling over the other in its efforts to get to her.

She had skinned her knee and the palm of her right hand but she felt nothing. Birds were shrieking now, a continuous outpouring of indignation and alarm. From higher in the tree a cascade of leaves floated from branch to branch, some landing on Jane as she manoeuvred to climb higher. A tree-frog startled her, his dull green colours blending with the leaves. She put out a hand and this time closed on a dead branch that collapsed and crashed to the ground.

For a freezing instant she thought she would fall. Her body swung out, her flailing hand arrested by a gigantic monkey rope. She used it for support then fell back against the massive trunk, her heart hammering in her breast. This was a terrible price to pay for delivering a screenplay. Lord knows she would have to stay in the tree until help arrived. Even that didn't make her happy. Perhaps she'd be looking down the barrel of a gun.

She sat down very carefully in the juncture of tree and branch, dangling her legs and wiping her sore hand on the underhem of her skirt. The scraped area was lightly embedded with bark and leaves. At least no unauthorised visitor to Monteverdi could claim they didn't get attention. There had to be plenty dead and buried around the place.

She rested her head exhaustedly against the curiously fragrant trunk taking deep breaths because she thought she would be sick. Could anything be more frightening than being held at bay by killer dogs? Strangely enough they were quieter now and as Jane lowered her head to look down she realised why.

Someone was riding a horse hell-for-leather down the drive, then horse and rider came into sight. Hadn't she known in her bones coming to Monteverdi was courting disaster?

He reined in abruptly and flung himself out of the saddle, thundering at the dogs to heel. His handsome face was intimidating in its cast, then he looked up and his expression changed abruptly to one of shock.

'For God's sake, Miss Gilmour, won't you tell me what you're doing up there?'

'I can't trust myself to speak, let alone move.'

'Just stay where you are.' His strong capable hands were already on the vines. He moved swiftly so within seconds he was propped against the trunk leaning towards her. 'Give me your hand.'

'No, thank you.'

'What's troubling you?'

'I'll be all right in a moment.' She spoke calmly but there was the faintest quivering in her deeply moulded mouth.

'I'm most humbly sorry you've been frightened.'

'Are you?' She dared to look into his brilliant, blue eyes.

'Don't be a little fool.' Deliberately he reached out and brushed a leaf from her shoulder. 'I thought you said you would ring before you honoured us with a visit?'

'Liz has got a migraine and my hire-car broke down.'

'If you'll allow me I can get you down very quickly.'

'You mean you're going to throw me?' she watched his eyes.

'For shame.' He slid his arm around her. 'All you have to do is cling.' His glance moved over her pale face to her delicate shoulders, her breast.

'I'm sorry. I don't think I can.'

'Why not?'

She stared up into his face, so close to him she could see the fine grain of his skin, breathe in his male fragrance. 'Those dogs, for instance.'

'I won't allow anything to hurt you.'

'Prove it.'

He held her slender wrist and turned away. 'Cicero, Caesar, *go home!*'

'They scared me half to death,' she whispered shakily.

'What do you think you did to me?' He lifted her slender body pinioning her. 'I hear this commotion and think it's some idiot who can't read and it's you stuck an awfully long way up a tree.'

'It's an awfully long way down.'

'Don't look,' he advised her. 'You've seen all that Tarzan stuff, haven't you?'

She nodded and somehow her mouth brushed his throat. 'What is it you have in mind?'

'I can get us to the ground in two minutes. I am aware your name is Jane.'

'You mean you're going to swing from those vines?'

'My dear Miss Gilmour,' he told her lightly, 'I grew up like Tarzan in the jungle. I already know you're a featherweight. All you have to do is cling and trust me.'

'Listen—' her voice rose slightly, 'can't we just climb down?'

'Chicken!' He laughed beneath his breath. She had never seen him laughing. He was devastating.

She put her arms around his neck and for the craziest second she thought he was going to kiss her. His blue eyes darkened and those sculptured features sharpened into sensuality. 'All right! Didn't you come up here for a bit of excitement?'

Never in her life had she placed her personal safety

so squarely in someone else's hands. Nevertheless it was breathless and it seemed to be over in a minute.

'Want to try it again?'

'One day.'

They were in each other's arms so someone coming up behind them would have thought they were lovers. Then abruptly his arms fell away. 'Okay?'

'Yes, thank you.' She began to flick out the folds of her skirt.

'You've hurt yourself.'

'Hmm.' She held out her palm for his inspection. 'I never noticed how much until now.'

'We'd do well to bathe that. And your knee.' He was speaking quietly yet the very air seemed to crackle. 'You have my most profound apologies. I wouldn't like to think what might have happened if you hadn't been so resourceful. Another woman might have been paralysed on the spot. I doubt it's any comfort for you to know the dogs would only have kept you bailed up. They are not killers. In fact, I'm very fond of them.'

'I'm never going to come here on foot.'

'Allow the dogs to get your scent and you need never fear them again.' He was looking down at her very directly, his lean height exaggerated in his riding-clothes.

She could feel the tremors running under her skin, but he obviously took it for nerves. 'Where is the car?' he asked swiftly.

'Fifteen minutes back.' She turned her blonde head. 'I think I ran out of petrol though the guage was registering a quarter in the tank. I locked it and the screenplay is inside.'

'I'm afraid bringing it to me has given you a harrowing time. 'The vibrant voice grated. 'I'll take you up with me on Sultan and arrange something when we get back to the house. I intend keeping you, you know that.'

'Keeping me?' Her green eyes were enormous and her slender neck snapped back.

'Just to be sure Miss Stoddart hurries back with her scriptwriter. If you intend shooting it will have to be completed before the onset of the monsoon. I'm sure your people know that. There is little time to be lost and you will be here to ensure Miss Stoddart gets things swiftly settled.'

'But you can't do that!'

'Oh, but I can,' he assured her smoothly. 'Have no fear, we will take proper care of you.'

'You're a . . .'

'What?'

To her surprise he looked down at her and smiled. It would have pierced any woman's armour, the curve of chiselled lips, the display of beautiful white teeth.

'A tyrant,' she said. Moreover he was totally unpredictable.

'Perhaps, a little.' He reached out and took her hand. 'Have you ever been up on a horse before?'

She went up on an easy fluid motion. 'Of course I have. Did anyone tell you you're tremendously strong?'

'I think I might have to be if we're going to see a lot of each other.' He gathered her back against him and shortened the reins. 'I'll make you a present of my favourite filly while you're here.'

'What do you want me to say?' She half turned her head only to pull back quickly at his overwhelming nearness.

'Why, thank you, I think.' He touched the sides of the magnificent, richly coloured chestnut and they moved off, gathering speed as the blood-horse got into stride.

His arm was strong and far too close to her breasts.

Was it possible he knew his physical aura ravished her? But it was exciting and strangely natural. The wind blew her hair but he didn't seem to mind though strands of it must have been wrapped around his throat.

They emerged from the trees following a wide path that skirted the house and led to the stables. On the upper balcony under the central arch of the triple-arched façade a young woman was standing. Antonella. It was impossible to see the expression on her face but Jane could well imagine what it would be. Horror, astonishment. How could anyone expect to see her sharing the saddle with a man who had every intention of keeping her a virtual captive?

An attendant ran out as they cantered into the courtyard with its bougainvillaea-wreathed walls and Alex McGovern dismounted before holding up his arms. In his blue eyes was a look of concentrated intensity that startled her so she slid down between his lean hard body and the warm, shining side of the horse, her slender body trembling.

'How is it you look so innocent, so sweet?'

She was so disturbed she couldn't answer. Only two days before he had been only a name, now she was afraid, afraid of the power he exerted. He had too much of everything. Power, wealth, courage, a sexual aura that made her body bend to him.

'Sandro?' It was Antonella's voice at its coldest and most insistent.

'Your cousin.' Jane looked up at him and flushed.

'So? Are you dreadfully frightened of her?'

'I think I'm more frightened of you.'

'I believe it.' There was no smile on his face but a flicker of sombre awareness. 'What really sent you here, I wonder? A job? God knows you're no ordinary little secretary.' A look of sudden bitterness crossed his face followed by a frown of impatience.

'Toni, what is it?' He turned, his height and breadth of shoulder shielding Jane so that she had time to smooth her hair and muster up some semblance of her habitual poise.

'What is Miss Gilmour doing here, and in such a way?' She sounded very angry.

'Her car broke down a few miles back. It's no cause for concern.'

'Perhaps.' Antonella reached them, a striking figure in a black and yellow zebra-print sun dress. 'How anyone can make so many errors!'

'I recall you had a car with a tendency to stop.'

'I was always forgetting to fill it with petrol, Sandro,' Antonella pouted. She motioned towards Jane's apricot skirt. There was a tear in the soft material where she had jerked it away from a sharp, projecting remnant of a dead branch. 'But so dishevelled, why?'

Jane could feel her anger rising. 'I think that's better forgotten. Perhaps as this looks like turning into a dramatic situation we could retrieve the screenplay. I'm tired and footsore and I have no relatives in this country to fall back on. I'm perfectly free to resign my job, but I don't want to. On the one hand I need the money and on the other I desperately want to help Liz.'

'Take it easy, Miss Gilmour.' Alex McGovern put his hand on her shoulder to settle her. 'I'm more than ever determined to read the screenplay and while I do so, by necessity, you're my guest. I realise you are being asked to give up your freedom, but it doesn't follow you won't enjoy yourself. You can go anywhere you like on the estate. You can ride, you can swim, play tennis, explore. There are any number of things you can decide to do but for the moment I think we'll take care of those grazes.'

'But where did she get them?' Antonella asked grimly.
'Climbing trees.'

'Sandro, you are teasing me.' She sounded to Jane's
way of thinking almost childishly aggrieved but she
looked so luscious, there was no other word, perhaps it
wouldn't make a great deal of difference whatever she
said.

All the way back to the house she kept up a flow of
Italian, and her cousin answered very briefly or not at
all. He spoke the language fluently as one might expect
and for all his Scottish ancestry at such times he
looked and acted every inch an Italian *marchese*. It
was a fascinating mix and Jane felt a sense of panic
that she should be so susceptible. Even now she was
allowing herself to be escorted like a privileged
prisoner under guard.

Helen McGovern met them at the front door, heard
Jane's story and took her kindly and firmly by the arm
to have her abrasions attended to before enjoying a
comforting cup of tea. 'We will have to replace that
pretty dress,' she told Jane apologetically. 'It's the
very least we can do.'

Antonella for her part had gone off with her cousin
to retrieve the all-important manuscript and Jane was
informed when they returned that the little runabout
had indeed run out of petrol. Worse, Antonella had
been obliged to drive it back as Alex McGovern was
much too tall to get into it.

It was impossible to tell what he was thinking as he
read through the screenplay. His handsome, dark face
remained cool and impenetrable, but when he finished
it there was an electric blue flare in his eyes.

'I'm afraid, Miss Gilmour, much of it won't do.'

Jane who had been pretending to read in the
armchair opposite him took a deep breath and willed
herself to remain calm and sensible.

'What is it you particularly object to, Mr McGovern?'

'The importance that has been attached to this governess. This love-affair almost leaps from the page. Ogilvie—he is attracted to her at once despite his wife by his side. Next you have her accepting the challenges of her rough new environment while the Contessa becomes a helpless neurotic. Ogilvie you have made appallingly ruthless. I know you have stressed the sophisticated veneer but nobody would be astonished at any act of violence. One can well see him getting rid of a woman he didn't want. There's no mystery here, there's implied murder!'

'Oh, no!'

'Please——' He stopped her with an imperious gesture. 'You've read this?'

'Of course.'

'And while I've been reading you've been intensely worried. Perhaps it's a great screenplay but it's impossible in this form. Everything that is known about my great-grandfather rejects a base action. So there was another woman in his life? A conniving little witch. His feelings for his wife remained the same. He built a palazzo to make her happy. To protect her. What is here is a whirlpool of strong, seething passions. You are aware Laura Hamilton is the heroine of your film?'

'She has a heroic, moving quality, yes.'

'This would cause my grandmother great grief.'

'I'm so sorry, but our screenplay is a work of fiction. I think it is very well accepted that the British did make wonderful colonists. They did adapt. It's also a British characteristic to thrive on challenges. John McGovern didn't send for an Italian governess for his children, he sent for an English one. It was his decision. Obviously he thought she might adapt better because he discovered his beautiful wife hadn't. It's common knowledge too John McGovern's Contessa was desperately unhappy in her primitive environment.'

'Setting the stage for a crime?'

'You know it doesn't read like that!' Jane cried pleadingly.

'Illicit lovers find ways of ridding themselves of hindrances.' He frowned blackly while he said it and looked down at the manuscript. 'You realise my grandmother and Antonella too are members of the Raffaelli family?'

'I had heard that of your cousin.'

'Who told you?' His blue gaze was very direct.

'Why, Helen—Mrs McGovern,' Jane gestured a little helplessly.

'Helen has taken a great liking to you,' he pointed out as though it was obvious she needed all the help she could muster.

'It's mutual. I like her very much too.'

'The character, Joseph, the islander,' he said abruptly. 'His descendants are still here.'

'Armstrong created a terrible problem sticking so closely to fact.'

'He did indeed.' The dark patrician face was contemptuous. 'The only suggestion I can make, Miss Gilmour, is you use your persuasive powers on your employer. She is an intelligent woman. She has a responsibility to you. It even seemed to me she had set herself up as your guardian while you're in this country. You're what, twenty, twenty-one?'

'Twenty-two.'

There was an odd look in his eyes. 'I simply can't allow you to go away until we get this thing straightened out. I think you do understand our point of view. You have a look of great sensitivity.'

'I understand, Mr McGovern,' Jane gave a small, unwitting sigh, 'but altering the script is outside my control. It's not entirely within Miss Stoddart's control. Perry Wyndham is an important man these days. He has only returned from America to direct this one film. He was very taken with the script.'

'And with you?'

Something in his voice made Jane flush. 'You seem to think I have ambitions as an actress?'

'I think you could be persuaded easily to play Laura Hamilton.'

'But that's crazy!' She sounded angry despite herself. 'I've had no training whatsoever. The thought has never occurred to me.'

'I'll bet it has occurred to Wyndham. We aren't so isolated that we haven't read of his marital and extra-marital exploits. Didn't he make his second wife a star?'

Jane looked down at her slender joined hands. 'I give you my firm assurance that I will not be playing Laura Hamilton. A recognised actress has already read the part. The highly accomplished Marina De Luca has practically begged to play the Contessa. Ogilvie will be played by an English actor, David Breeden, you would know him. He's an international star.'

'In short,' he said curtly, 'it has all been worked out.'

At his tone Jane's beautiful skin turned to marble. 'It's terribly important we have your approval and co-operation.'

'You mean you need Monteverdi?'

'Yes,' she said simply. 'There couldn't be a more beautiful or more authentic location. Not all of the film will be shot on location of course. Many of the scenes, especially those involving the children, will be shot at our studios in Sydney. It would be the most tremendous help to us if we had your co-operation.'

'In any case if you delay your filming you will be overtaken by the monsoon season. I doubt very much if you've ever experienced a cyclone.'

'No.' She shook her blonde head. 'It's glorious at the moment.'

'All that will change. When it rains here, it really rains. I'm sure there will be a cyclone or two to keep us on our toes. What I propose to do now is drive you back to town so you can pack your things and while you're doing that I'll make my wishes known to Miss Stoddart. If she's too ill to speak to me, I'm sure you can convince her we must arrive at a compromise. Having you stay with us will hasten negotiations.'

Two days later Liz returned to Sydney on a regular jet flight and Jane became a guest of Alex McGovern. Helen, for one, was genuinely pleased. 'It's nice to have company,' she told Jane warmly. 'I do so miss my daughters. Rachael lives in California. She met her husband when he was big-game fishing on the Barrier Reef. They're a wine-growing family, and Susan has the travel bug. At the moment she's in Greece.'

'You live on Monteverdi, Helen?' Jane asked. They were sitting in the atrium, drinking coffee and enjoying the spectacle of the orchids in full bloom.

'No, dear.' Helen looked surprised. 'Nonna—you will meet her tonight—invited us here for Antonella's stay. Also she suffered a slight heart-attack some months ago and she likes her family near her. She never got over the death of her adored son.'

'Alex's father?' Jane had only just been persuaded to call him by his Christian name. *Marchese* seemed more appropriate.

'Yes.' Helen looked sad. 'Douglas was cut down in

the prime of life. He was killed going to a friend's aid during one of our worst cyclones. Power lines had come down.'

'Please, Helen, don't distress yourself.' Jane reacted quickly to the shimmer of tears.

'No.' Momentarily Helen bowed her head in her hand. 'It was a terrible tragedy. We all went to pieces for a while. Douglas was the most *vital* man. It seems inconceivable he's gone. He'd been doing incredibly daring things all his life. We couldn't take it in. Only for Alex, Sandro, as she calls him, did Nonna bring herself back from the grave. She worships him. Alex is his father's son.'

'And his mother?'

Helen of the direct gaze looked away. 'Bella was shattered. She lives abroad these days and Alex visits her at least twice a year. She never did get on with Nonna and afterwards: the whole relationship fell apart. Alex was a young man well able to take control of his heritage so Bella . . . went.'

'She must miss them, husband, son.'

'My dear child, I honestly don't know how she survived. She was and is very beautiful but she never remarried. Now, I see I've made you sad. That can't be. Tell me about your own family. I can see you've come from a very loving home.'

If Jane had expected to meet a mellowed old lady at dinner she would have been in for a considerable surprise.

As it was she expected an Italian matriarch in the grand tradition and she wasn't disappointed. In the whole course of her twenty-two years she had never met such a family. The Signora was the household staff called her, had all her grandson's imperiousness and then more. She was tiny but stiffly upright, her olive cheeks were sunken but she still bore the vestiges of great beauty. Her hair was pure white and copious in contrast to her still-black eyes and she wore the most strangely antiquated clothes that made no concession to time, place or climate. Only her age made her vulnerable for her presence was strong.

'Antonella told me you were beautiful in the English way. You are,' she told Jane in a voice that was harsh and almost as heavily accented as Antonella's. It occurred to Jane it was also hostile.

'Thank you for allowing me to stay in your beautiful home, Signora,' Jane responded, but the old lady waved her away.

'A prisoner, no? A prisoner of my grandson.'

Yet dinner wasn't the agonising ordeal Jane expected. The McGoverns were much travelled, cultured people and the Signora herself was a woman of considerable sharp wit. Only Antonella refused to join in the general conversation, resorting to her now-familiar impersonation of a smouldering volcano.

Immediately dinner was over, the Signora abandoned them abruptly, motioning to Antonella to follow her to her suite of rooms. All of them had risen and now Alex McGovern took Jane by the elbow, fulfilling an earlier promise to show her over what was a very large house.

'I'm sure you won't be able to take it all in at once, Jane,' Helen called, while her husband comfortably ensconced on the sofa beside her looked up and smiled. 'Steer clear of the fountains. One can only properly view them in bathing dress.'

'What does that mean?' Jane asked lightly as they moved away from the large sitting-room where they had been enjoying coffee.

'I'll surprise you another time. When I was a child nothing made me happier than to see all the fountains turned on at once.' An amused smile flickered about his finely chiselled lips. 'Now, I think we should start at the front of the house. The main drawing-room or the Grand Salone is much too grand for the family to use when we are on our own. The same applies to the formal dining-room. It is only used for very special occasions but they are wonderful rooms when they are all filled up as they are when we entertain on a large scale. When my father was alive we had friends, family, staying from all parts of the world. There were parties galore. My mother is a very beautiful, calm and gentle woman but my father was a vivid, vital man like no other. He drew people to him like a magnet. He was enormously popular not simply because of his wealth and generosity but because of the breadth and scope of his personality. This great house was never empty when my father was alive.'

'You miss him terribly.'

'It is not a thing I can normally discuss.'

'I understand,' Jane said gently, 'but you have your wonderful memories.'

He nodded, very sombrely. 'He was always helping someone.'

'For a man like that there must have been no other choice.'

'No.' He looked down at her for a long minute and his blue eyes glittered like jewels in a bronze mask. 'What is it they say? Greater love hath no man than he lays down his life for another? You can see the family pride? It should make it easier for you to appreciate your film will not be made unless your people accept our terms. We could hold you up indefinitely until the project became too expensive, too difficult to handle.'

His tone was so daunting Jane reached forward a little blindly coming into contact with the brass door-handle. She began to turn it but as she did so his lean, long-fingered hand closed over hers. 'Come, I'm sorry,' he said in a voice so different it was almost a caress. 'I didn't mean to speak so sharply to you but that is only because you make me feel things I don't want to.'

The door didn't give and momentarily Jane was held captive within the half-circle of his arm. Sensation flooded over her, so acute it was distressing.

'It would be a lot easier if we turned the lock,' he suggested. 'What is it about me that makes you tremble?'

'If you must know it's your arrogance,' Jane said in a muffled tone.

'Really?' He sounded amused. His face was now so close to hers she could smell the faint, tangy aroma of his aftershave. 'For my part, I find it enchanting a woman could be so vulnerable in this feminist age.'

'Let us say you're my most intimidating male to date.'

'Intimidating?' There was an attractive break in his voice. 'This is not the way I wish to present myself to you.'

'Perhaps not, but you seem to belong to that special breed of men who automatically inherit the earth.'

'All this simply because I seek to protect my family.' His downbent glance was so insistent she had to look at him. He could seize and capture any woman he wanted.

'I thought that, before there was ever a word between us.'

He put out a hand and to her shock brushed her cheek. 'And why would you need words with the legacy of those eyes?'

She was intoxicated with him, made unguarded, dazzled, the touch of his fingers still on her cheek though his hand had long fallen.

They toured the Grand Salone, he pointing out this

or that family heirloom, she continually asking
questions, the atmosphere between them so shivery it
could never be called companionable. Yet Jane was
enormously interested in all that she saw. He had the
knack of bringing the past alive, of making it seem like
yesterday so she thought if she turned her head very
quickly she might find him dressed in the male
splendour of another age. One moment he was very
much the modern dynamo, another the focus of a long
and illustrious heritage. Jane had never met such a
vibrant human being though her fascination was
tempered by the certain knowledge he was anything
but gentle. He was proud, arrogant, high-mettled, a
complex study in male power. She was as much torn
by excitement as desperately anxious to protect
herself. No matter what anyone said, very many
women made a man their whole life, whereas men,
accepting this state of affairs as entirely natural,
tended to think of women as an outside interest. One
reason Jane had remained a virgin so long was that she
so strongly believed the gift of her body was the
ultimate act of love. She wanted nothing but a deep,
caring relationship so it bothered her now to find
herself so violently attracted to a near-stranger. It was
like moving around in an alien landscape.

In the yellow drawing-room, so-called because of
the beautiful silk-lined walls, hung a huge, magnificent
painting of a young woman in full evening-dress.
Materials of satin and lace were sumptuous. She wore
pearls, ropes of them, a triple choker displaying a large
ruby clasp surrounded by diamonds, others falling
below her waist. The standing figure was arranged
before ornate marble columns with a moonlit sky and a
tracery of trees adding drama to the background and
illuminating the exquisite skin tones and the white and
silver of the dress, but all one really saw was the eyes.

They dominated the painting, gazing down in the most life-like and melancholy way. They were huge and black and they belonged to a beautiful woman who undoubtedly had been unhappy at the time of the sitting. They were acutely disturbing and Jane with her sensitive antennae was convinced the painted lady was trying to say something. For all her wealth and beauty happiness had abandoned her.

Jane couldn't help herself. She moved closer, staring up. The artist had been a master but she was unable to decipher the scrawl at the bottom right-hand corner of the great canvas. It was a painting in the classical tradition and it aroused in Jane deep emotions.

'How sad she is!' she murmured with the utmost tenderness. 'How sad and empty.'

'I beg your pardon.'

His deep voice startled her. 'Can't you see it?' she turned quite urgently realising with a ripple of dismay he looked impossibly aloof.

'I see loneliness, vulnerability.'

'She's trying to say something.'

'You realise whom you are looking at?'

'Of course, the Contessa.' Jane nodded her blonde head. 'It may have been painted in her own world, but the eyes look alienated.'

'You have some training in psychiatry?' he asked crisply.

'I have a capacity for divining the unhappiness of others.'

He looked down at her, the light glancing off her gilded head. 'You're saying the Contessa was not happy in her marriage?'

She considered this gravely. 'Who knows what goes on inside a marriage? Her eyes are so melancholy, so full of sorrow.'

'So of course you have reached the conclusion her husband was responsible?'

His hostility slashed at her, giving her actual physical pain. 'No, no, I'm not saying——'

'You're saying the Contessa was unhappy, tormented because her husband was unfaithful. Surely that's how you intend to play it?'

'Please, don't be angry.' She put her pale, slender fingers on his sleeve. 'Life is critical, isn't it? At any moment one can turn the wrong corner. All my life I've felt safe and happy but things happen.'

'You mean at any time one can make a catastrophic error of judgment? Like falling in love with the wrong woman?' His downbent glance was turbulent, ocean-blue.

'Didn't John McGovern marry his children's governess?'

'So?' He looked very foreign and fascinating.

'He must have loved her.'

There was instantly anger and arrogance in his face. 'I would say he chose to protect what was left of her good name.'

'Mightn't he have sent her back to England?' she asked him in some distress. 'Why are you denying he loved her?'

'Because he didn't,' he returned emphatically. 'Is love a wild attraction?'

'Love is wild, surely.'

'And what would you know of it?' he demanded tersely, danger prowling in his eyes. 'You have the innocent air of a virgin, a lovely but inexperienced green girl. Unlike many I think you would find it very shocking to give your body without love, so undoubtedly passion has not touched you.'

'Has it touched you?'

He looked straight into her lustrous green eyes. 'A

man is different from a woman. You know that, little one. I am used to love affairs.'

She recovered enough of her poise to shrug. 'You do look as though you have plenty of passion to spare.' She calmed herself further by turning nonchalantly away, shaken in the next moment to have him block her path.

'I think it is quite possible to begin a love affair with you.'

'Your arrogance amazes me!' In fact she was half mesmerised by his mocking expression.

'I think you've been half expecting me to kiss you since the moment we met.'

'I'm sure you're going to try.'

'On the contrary, I'm only teasing you. You fascinate me as a study.'

'Shall we look at the rest of the house?' she suggested coolly, at the same time giving an involuntary little shudder.

'Wouldn't you like a look at the garden? We could walk down to the beach.' From anger and arrogance his blue eyes were dancing with amused mockery.

'Surely the beach is a place for a sunny day.'

'You know it's magic by moonlight. You're frightened as well, aren't you?'

'I know you've led a feudal life up here and I'm a hostage.'

'Histrionics! You know I would never hurt you.' He held out his hand, body and mind reaching for her, locking her into his own pattern.

Multiple anxieties crowded into her consciousness yet she went with him. She knew she shouldn't, yet she discovered too late she couldn't bear to let go of his hand. He was too painfully tantalising to her, a man who expected always to have any woman he wanted. In just such a way could that first McGovern have drawn an innocent young woman into a forbidden trap. Behind the civilised veneer lurked the ancient law.

Yet as an experience it was ravishing. The gardens were glorious, beautifully lit and floating their myriad flower scents, heady, tropical perfumes. Once when she trembled, he stopped abruptly and asked her if she were cold. Curious how concerned for her he sounded.

The air was like silk. If she trembled it was because a current of high feeling was pulsing between them that made normal, light conversation almost impossible. They were duelling with each other but one was infinitely more skilful.

They reached the edge of the lawn looking out at the wide shining crescent of sand and the entrancing sight of a huge copper moon laying a golden path across the rippling waters. It was so brilliantly lit, so seemingly solid, Jane had the impression one could almost walk across it. A light wind blew off the sea and she turned her face this way and that as long silvery skeins of her hair wound across her throat and eyes.

'You should have worn a scarf.' He gave a low laugh and put out his hand, grasping her long hair into a golden rope.

She fought the queer craving to surrender to his magic. 'It's a pleasure to have the breeze in my hair.'

'And of course you are aware it's extraordinarily seductive.'

'Please stop.'

'Stop what?' He laughed again.

'You've got to.'

'All right, *piccola*. I am yours to command.'

He dropped his hand just as she jerked her head and she gave a little protesting cry. 'That hurt.'

'You did it yourself.'

The breeze was cool against her heated skin. She

moved away thinking of the pleasure of going into those shimmering waves, of swimming in water turned to midnight silk. There was a nightbird somewhere whistling. A strange cascade of notes that seemed to add to her urgency. She liked her life the way it was; serene and secure, not crowded with new and dangerous sensation. Passion wrecked lives and she had the terrifying notion he had only to kiss her to stir up hungers that could only appal her. Fate moved people like pawns. Now. Long ago.

Her beautiful hair blew like a banner and the freshening sea-wind moulded her thin dress to the contours of her body. The breeze brought with it scents of the islands, so warm and spicy they became sparkles in the blood.

'You can't be serious?' he called to her.

It was crazy, her mad flight. She paused and looked back. He was very tall and he was turning her very bones fluid.

'I thought this was meant to be a quiet stroll?'

'With some people it might be.'

'Ah—so you are admitting we disturb one another?'

'I believe you are doing your best to disturb me.'

'Oddly enough, I am.' He reached out a hand and she gave a little cry.

'This is very rash of you, isn't it?' she challenged him, her spirit on fire but her senses in an inexorable whirl. 'I've formed the strong opinion your family would like to see you married to Antonella.'

'Surely you're joking?' He was holding, smoothing, caressing her delicate shoulders.

'Not at all.' She stared up at him, watching carefully for any hint of reaction.

'And it's incumbent on me to do as others want?' He smoothed his palm down the satiny side of her face.

'I've read your love for your grandmother in your eyes. You would do anything to make her happy.'

This seemed to arrest him. 'To be perfectly serious, I would. Anything except marry a woman I didn't love.'

Every nerve in her body was reacting to the pressure of his hands. 'Antonella loves you.'

'Is that any of your business?' he demanded sardonically.

'I expect it's hers, if you intend to amuse yourself with me, always supposing I am even vulnerable. I mean, is it really worth it?'

Staring into his gleaming eyes she knew it was.

'So why don't we see?' he suggested gently. 'It's been a kind of agony keeping my hands off you.'

The sensuality of his words turned her limp. She seemed to sway towards him, yet so complex was her reaction, combining acute sexual arousal with an elemental resistance to domination, a second wave of strength rushed for her. Her free hand, her only weapon, came up, but instead of overwhelming her with his vastly superior physical strength, he stepped away from her like a trained athlete amused at the unequal struggle.

'All at once she fights me!' He turned up his hands and gave a low, mocking laugh.

'And why not? I'm a person with a mind of my own, not an object to be manipulated at will.'

'You don't want me to touch you?'

'No!'

'I had the distinct impression you did.'

Night engulfed them. 'All I want is to finish this walk!' she declared jaggedly.

'So be it! Such a pity you shed your pretty sandals. The soldier crabs come out at night. Legions of the little devils. You could get a nasty nip.'

'What?' Her gaze flew around the dazzling sand, and woman-like she grasped at his sleeve. 'You could have told me before.'

'The only reason was to get you back in my arms.'

She was consumed by a heat she never thought possible. 'I'll scream, I promise you. I'll have them all running from the house.'

He turned her fully into his arms. 'You will not demean yourself, nor me. I have listened to what you've said and you'd better know now I'm not amusing myself. Most likely I'm creating havoc for us both.'

She felt an answering surge of apprehension. 'Alex, please.'

'Say that again. The way you speak my name fascinates me.'

'You can turn back now.'

'When everything about you is reaching out for me?' He grasped her hair, tilting her head back, and every thought of resistance fled her. She might very well suffer for this but she could not be without his kiss.

He lowered his head, catching her half-open mouth with such ardour she turned weightless within his encircling arms. She was ravaged.

Abruptly before she went under she wrenched her mouth aside. 'Alex!'

'It's all right.'

It wasn't. She was dizzy, all strength moving out of her weak and helpless body. He had her enfolded now and for the first time in her life she wanted more than anything to have this ecstasy continue, to have his hands touch her breasts, the silken intimate parts of her body. She could not get enough.

Her throat arched as his mouth travelled downwards, the effect of such pleasure as ungovernable as a narcotic in the blood. She wanted shockingly to remove all barriers between them, to feel instead of layers of material, warm flesh.

When at last his strong hand shaped her breast, the shock was so enormous she moaned and tried to gulp in deep breaths of air. The moment had no precedent. She had never felt so wild, nor experienced her own passionate femaleness so close to her.

'Alex, please stop!' He was arousing in her eroticism she couldn't bear to feel.

'My God, how can you expect me to?' His vibrant voice was a low growl. He forced her back over his arm, her nipples swelling like buds to his touch. 'How beautiful you are,' he groaned. 'The lovely shape of your breasts, of your body was my first memory of you. A golden water-nymph.'

She was shaking now so that she could hardly stand, but she could not stop him, slow, strong vibrations starting deep within her, spreading convulsively. She was as weak as any other woman caught in the grip of unending desire.

'Gianina . . .' His hard male body was profoundly aroused, so daunting in its raw power she could not ignore it.

She was almost whimpering now with the force of pleasure and he slid his mouth over hers, filling his nostrils with their combined scents, deepening the pressure, drinking from her open mouth as though he found it incredibly luscious.

Her heart fluttered in pain and her eyelids plunged. Their bodies were in such urgent contact she felt as though she were slipping over the verge into possession. Was it possible to be consumed by such high emotions? She was as scorched as if exposed to a naked sun.

When his hand brushed down over her body, she jerked back, a primitive fear asserting itself. If she allowed any further intimacies she could no longer contain herself. She could even black out.

'You've wanted this,' she uttered fiercely. 'You've expected it. Surely it's gone far enough.'

He drew back immediately, his hand on the underside of her chin. 'Why are you hissing at me so fiercely, little one? There is no one to hear us. See us.'

'I'm not happy about any of these things!' Yet spasm after spasm of emotion racked her.

'I would never hurt you,' he returned quietly. 'I am trying very hard to make myself gentle. You are a virgin, aren't you?'

'Yes,' she said with the air of someone who almost had to defend herself. 'I don't know if you understand or not, but the act of love is terribly important to me.'

'Why would it not be for a woman?' he returned forcefully. 'A woman's role is altogether different. She must receive a man into her body, permit possession, while the man needs only to be moved to aggression. A man should be dominant, little one. He has to be, but I would never force myself upon an unwilling woman. Your innocence for the moment protects you. You sound defensive about being a virgin. I like it. It's precisely what I want my woman to be. No matter how much your Women's Lib exploits you, virginity in a young woman will always be deeply desirable.

'Yet you would take me this minute if I let you,' she challenged him.

'I would not!' he said in clipped tones. 'I'll admit you evoke a tempest in me but I'm not about to force you down on the sand. Outwardly you look so cool but your own sensuality has come as a surprise. Do you think I didn't feel your fright?'

'Passion is very scary.'

'I guess it is.' He stared over her head, his brilliant eyes shadowed. 'I thought I knew all about it.'

Jane shook her blonde head. 'It occurs to me you do. *I* don't. It seems I'm in the wrong place at the wrong time.'

'So.' A freshening wind had blown up and he took off his light jacket and put it around her shoulders. 'You have my assurance I won't even kiss you again until you've had time to catch up.'

A wonderful relaxing warmth enveloped her. 'You're making fun of me.'

'Well, just a little.' He put his arm around her as they retraced their steps to the terraced lawn.

'I don't want an affair, Alex,' she whispered.

'An affair is too easy. I've never met a woman I couldn't hold back from.'

'We've got completely different lives. Tonight was a mistake.'

'So why do you sound so unhappy?' He made her sit on the low stone wall while he slid her narrow feet into her shoes.

'I'm really quite all right.' She had an overwhelming compulsion to lean forward and kiss him.

'There's nothing dishonourable about my wanting to make love to you, Gianina.' His fingers encircled her slim ankle. 'I have no wife, no fiancée. You are committed to no one and I understand completely your feelings. A man always thinks more of a woman who values herself.'

'Even when he hopes to seduce her?' she asked wryly, stretching out her hand to touch his thick, springy hair. 'I do think you're a master sorcerer, but I trust you as well.'

He looked up at her very suddenly. 'Don't always trust me, Gianina. I'm not super-human.'

'Have you ever made love to Antonella?'

'What kind of man would I be to tell?'

'I suppose I'm trying to protect myself.'

'So, Toni and I have slept together.' His blue eyes turned dark. 'I say this: I did not seduce her. It was no plan on my part, forgive me. Toni has been reared to believe that what she wants she must have.'

'And she wanted you for a lover.'

He looked at her ironically. 'What is a woman anyway? One year a playful little girl, the next hell-bent on adult adventures. Toni is young but she knows very well what she's doing. She's very sexy and determined. I'm well aware I'm not the only man she's tried to bring under her control.'

'My God!' Jane's mind was reeling. She stood up. 'If you want proof she really loves you, you'd better look into those bottomless eyes.'

'You asked me to tell you,' he said quietly. 'I could have lied.'

'I had no right to ask anything at all. This is all deeply personal, yet sometimes the truth is the only protection. Your cousin could be rather terrifying in her jealousy.'

'I will allow nothing to happen to you.' He gripped her arm and drew her to him. She could feel the anger and the tremendous energy in him.

'Your grandmother is extremely fond of Antonella.'

He shrugged his powerful shoulders. 'She has looked on her as a granddaughter. She nursed her as a baby. I am fond of Toni myself. Her parents' lifestyle has not been in her best interests. She learnt too much, too soon. In many ways I pity my little cousin.'

'So, failing some catastrophic encounter, you might have found it quite tolerable to marry her?' Jane had a peculiar sick feeling at the pit of her stomach, like someone who inadvertently was splitting two people apart.

He reacted immediately to the self-condemnation in her voice. 'On the contrary, little one,' he said curtly, 'I've been waiting to find my own wife.'

CHAPTER FOUR

JANE awoke the next morning wondering if she could have dreamt the night before. It was so far from her safe and relaxed life it had the aura of some dark fantasy. Had Alex McGovern made love to her so passionately? Had she really responded like a woman who had ultimately found the satisfaction she craved? Tentatively she touched her mouth. It was still faintly swollen. It was all real and she had the frightening notion she would never be able to obliterate the effects of one dangerous hour.

When they had returned to the house, Antonella had been waiting for them, her great black eyes burning with jealous hostility. It was obvious she knew something had happened between them but if she expected to bring her lover—ex-lover—to heel she failed. Alex stopped and spoke to her and while Jane continued on upstairs the two of them returned to the atrium, Antonella speaking in her own language and Alex answering in an easy, assured tone. Only a fool could believe two such sensual and exotic creatures would remain on a familial level. In fact their relationship wasn't all that close, but a kinship. No wonder the Signora was wary of Jane. Many a family had been torn apart by a rash and defiant love affair. Jane reminded herself she wouldn't be on Monteverdi for long even if life away from it might seem endless.

Through the open window she could see a cloudless blue sky yet a white, steaming mist ringed the pinnacle of the plantation's jagged monolith. Tangled in her mind were fragments of her dreams. A woman had

been in them, a beauty: a crown of raven-coloured
hair, an ivory skin and inky pools for eyes. Jane
shivered although the early morning was blissfully
warm. The woman had been the Contessa and the man,
though the Contessa's husband, had been Alex
McGovern, with a harder, tauter, more ruthless
expression. Once half waking she had turned her head
to see him standing beside her bed. Icy consciousness
had flown over her and Jane had woken up. Like then,
she sat up in bed clutching her heart. Did strong
passions live on in the atmosphere? Certainly the
Contessa's tragedy had clouded many lives.

Jane was beginning to discover in herself a craving
to know the truth. Were there no writings, no diaries?
Something that would surrender up a clue to that
tragic disappearance? Once in her dream she had seen
a white hand rising from a dark sheet of water.
Monteverdi was a jungle even now. What must it have
been like in those early days of the colony when slaves
had worked the sugar fields? Was a crazed labourer a
demon or simply a simple, coloured man who had
been driven mad? His blood had flowed for
punishment had been meted out without the benefit of
any court.

Jane's melancholy thoughts were interrupted by a
rain of pebbles against the white shutters. One flew
into the room and landed on the jewel-coloured
Kashan rug. She leapt out of bed and shoved her arms
into her white, ribbon-striped robe. Her balcony
overlooked an emerald swathe of lawn and a lily-
strewn reflection pond and she walked out and looked
over.

Alex McGovern dressed in riding-clothes was
standing beneath her, so handsome Jane felt a sharp
sense of despair, his blue gaze as vivid as summer
lightning.

'Didn't you tell me you could ride?'

She stared down at him, startled. 'Why, certainly I did, but you can't mean now?'

'I wouldn't be paying you this early-morning visit without a reason. I do mean now.'

She sank back a little, anxieties fluttering around her. Her body wanted to go but her mind was sending out urgent warnings.

'Jane?'

'I'm here,' she called after a little time.

'I'm coming up.'

It was delivered with some force and Jane flew to the balustrde, her heart jumping as she saw him catch hold of a magnificent climbing King Jasmine.

'Look, Alex, please.'

'You make a timorous little Juliet up there on your balcony.'

'For God's sake! That vine could break.'

He didn't answer but moved steadily upwards, superbly fit and totally unpredictable.

'What's so important about coming up?' She flung herself backwards as he put one long jodhpured leg over the balcony.

'I saw your face cloud up. What is it?'

He advanced on her like some splendid devouring panther and Jane pushed so hard back into the wall she hit her head.

'My dear girl, are you hurt?' He stopped in front of her, one hand holding her shoulder.

In fact she saw a couple of stars. 'If it's worth anything to you, you're a very daunting man.'

'And you're terrified you were created just for me?' His voice was filled with life and mockery. 'I simply wanted to be sure you would come with me.' His blue eyes were moving over every inch of her, the slip of a white nightdress, the loose matching robe, the way she put her blonde hair in a thick plait for bed. 'As well I know now you're as beautiful first thing in the morning as any woman could wish to be.'

'And you're certainly an expert!' Her green eyes suddenly sparkled. 'What if anyone should come to the door?'

'I'll take you down on the vine.'

'All this playing at Lord of the Jungle.' It was easier to keep talking than meet his eyes. Talk was her salvation, when she only wanted one thing. Falling in love was all-consuming. It was almost impossible to think of anything else.

'Stop trembling,' he said gently. 'I'm not going to touch you. Dressed like that I'm damned sure I couldn't release you.' There was a brilliant, challenging glint in his eyes. 'You're as high-strung as a thoroughbred filly.'

'I seem to be, with you around.' She stared a little desperately past his shoulder, the sun on the thick golden rope of her hair. 'I'd love to go riding, Alex, but something tells me it could be stupid.'

'You want to retreat into your safe little world?'

She took a deep breath and risked a look at him. 'I don't want to make an enemy of your grandmother. I don't really want to hurt Antonella. I am not another woman.'

His face turned as hard and ruthless as the face in her dream. Her green eyes opened wide and for an instant she was impaled with shock. He seemed to lunge forward grabbing her wrist and pulling her into the bedroom, whirling her around in front of him so that her robe billowed out and he could see her slender near-naked body beneath.

'I wonder why I need a sermon when I mean you no harm. If you attempt to raise your voice I'll shout you down. If you attempt to fight me I promise you I'll find some riding-gear and dress you myself.'

'You're absolutely crazy!' She threw out her hand but he ducked.

'Is it so terrible to want to see the plantation through your eyes? Green as a little cat's.' He lunged again and clasped her own arm around her.

'Just let me go!'

'If you could, you'd run like hell. You're frightened, Jane, aren't you? What do you expect I'll do with you?'

'Everything!' she panted.

'I would no more hurt you than I would any beautiful, innocent little creature.' He brought down his head, his mouth very close to her ear. 'If I let you go will you get dressed?'

She barely nodded and he lifted the heavy plait off her nape and kissed it. 'Good girl!' His brilliant eyes glowed. 'The fresh air will do you good. From the look of you I'd say you've had a tense night.'

She was so agitated she couldn't find her breath.

'Do you mind if I use the door?' He looked mockingly into her widened eyes. 'Ah, it's locked. There's absolutely no reason why you should do that, Jane.'

'Not when you're so expert at climbing vines.'

'There's another fascinating thing about this house,' he told her before he withdrew. 'Secret doorways and panels. Who knows, there might be one in this very room.'

Jane determined she would check that out another time. Now she moved in an excited flurry catching up a soft cream shirt and yellow jeans. She couldn't even begin to consider the consequences of her actions. All she knew was where he beckoned, she followed.

When he saw her he raised a slightly mocking

eyebrow. 'If it's possible you look even more feminine dressed like a boy.'

'Confidentially I think jeans suit me.'

'Oh, they do!'

'And they are practical as I don't intend to ride side-saddle.'

'You can ride, I hope.' He looked up at the peacock-blue sky and spread his arms wide. A pagan prince in his kingdom.

'Lead the way.' All of a sudden she was very relaxed. There was no need to tell him she had been riding since earliest childhood. He already knew she loved horses from that one ride when he had had his arm so tightly around her. Their bodies had moved in unison like a perfectly matched pair.

The filly that emerged from under the bougainvillaea-shadowed archway was as beautiful as it was possible for a horse to be; pure-bred Arab with a coat like a newly minted gold coin and a silvery white mane and tail. A palomino, the golden horse of Spain and one of the world's most sought-after riding horses.

'She's gorgeous!' Jane locked her hands together in admiration.

'You like her?' His answering smile was indulgent.

'Who wouldn't?'

'Her name is Melitta.'

'She's not Antonella's horse, by any chance?'

'What of it?' The handsome face looked haughty.

'I'd prefer not to ride Antonella's horse. She wouldn't like it.'

'It is not Antonella's horse,' he said crisply. 'That's a fact. Antonella does not ride. She tried once, took a spill and refused to try again.'

Jane went forward and patted the palomino's nose, moving her hand to its satiny neck. 'You should have made her. Everyone takes a spill.'

'She was very adamant,' he said, more easily. 'I would have persisted only horses don't play a part in Antonella's everyday life. She is very much a city creature. The weeks she spends with us are when she is recuperating from the high life.'

'And I suppose you visit her?'

He gave her a leg up. 'You know I have many relations in Rome, Venice, Florence. They look after me well.'

Afterwards Jane couldn't recall such an exhilarating experience. They rode through the jade streams of cane, traversing a bridge over a wide expanse of lagoon and coming down on the private forest. There was no need to lower their heads. The trees were giants and widely spaced so they could go fast through the trails.

Once there had been a solid wall of trees but they had been cleared and now it was a marvellous cultivated wood, dreamlike in its beauty and eternal coolness. From time to time they slowed down and rode side by side in a kind of rapt companionship. It was a wonderful understanding that existed between people who loved horses and handled them beautifully.

When he urged her down on to the beach she followed, riding the firm sand then taking the horses out into the waves, all of them, man, woman, animals revelling in the tingling freshness, the astringent wind and the fabulous warmth of the sun.

Intoxicated, happy, Jane leaned back in the saddle, eyes closed, and in the next instant he closed the big bay beside her, seizing her around her narrow waist and kissing her until she was flushed and panting.

She felt totally unable to withstand him, yet she tried. 'Next time I'll remember not to shut my eyes.'

There were brilliant, devil-glints in his laughing glance. 'You can't do what you do and expect not to be kissed. Come sailing with me, Gianina. We could disappear for days.'

'Indeed we could,' she said sternly. 'Afterwards is another matter.' Rapture turned to tragedy. It had happened before. Jane touched the filly's sides and the beautiful little animal shot off.

Far away, up at the house with its commanding view of the bay, a woman stood with powerful fieldglasses to her eyes. The cords of her neck were taut and her hands were so tightly clenched the small knuckles showed white.

'She wants him,' the woman gritted. 'She wants my Sandro.'

So much happened in a week. He took her everywhere, brushing aside every obstruction until the whole household was thin with tension. Liz phoned repeatedly but it wasn't until the following Monday that she returned to Monteverdi with powerful reinforcements.

Jane moved back quietly while the introductions went on.

'My colleagues, Perry Wyndham, our internationally famous director, Bryan Rowland, my co-producer and the man responsible for our screenplay.'

Alex's grandmother sat in a throne-like antique chair, glancing maliciously around the circle of faces. She was obviously in pain from an arthritic condition but succeeded in appearing impressively severe. Liz had already given Bryan a poke in the ribs as he gazed about with open-mouthed attention and even Perry, grown incredibly blasé from his years in America was visibly impressed.

Everywhere one looked from the coffered and painted ceilings, around the richly hung walls, past the magnificent Carrara marble fireplace to the parqueted floor complemented by the muted brilliance of Savonnerie rugs, was something to gape at or speculate on its worth.

'Your home is magnificent, Mr McGovern,' Perry remarked warmly. 'It will look splendid on film.'

Alex McGovern absorbed this with remote charm. 'Which is what we are here to discuss.' His voice was cool and rather foreign. 'I think you'll agree we have looked after Miss Gilmour well.'

'Yes, indeed! She looks wonderful!' Liz cried with hoarse gaiety. The Signora's cold, brooding gaze was making her feel rather insecure. 'That tan is marvellously effective with ash-gold hair and green eyes.'

Perry Wyndham turned his head. 'I only wish Jane had some experience as an actress. She'd be perfect as Laura Hamilton. I don't like this Graham girl one little bit. She's too obvious.'

'It will be different when she really enters into the role,' Liz said with certainty. 'We must give her a chance.'

'You've brought the revised screenplay?' Alex McGovern asked crisply, noting the amount of attention Perry Wyndham was giving Jane's gilded face and loosened cloud of blonde hair.

'Of course.' Liz lifted her arm. 'Bryan's worked very hard on it. Would it be at all helpful if we ran through the particular scene that was so much in question?'

'It will call for a damned good actress,' Bryan interrupted almost sourly. 'I was so restricted in what I could say.'

'Shall we hear it?' the old lady suggested tightly. 'Who is going to read? You, Miss Stoddart?'

'Bryan and I would be glad to.' Liz was grateful for Helen McGovern's sympathetic expression. As for the rest of them, they looked like the Borgias.

'Such consideration!' the Signora mocked. 'Roberto, a glass of water to my hand, please.'

Robert McGovern sprang up dutifully and when he returned Bryan began to read,

'What's the matter with you, can't you sleep?'

It was an important scene, the first big scene between Ogilvie and the governess. Night. And Ogilvie had come on his children's governess pacing the terrace in obvious discomposure.

'I'm sorry, sir, did I disturb you?' Liz's ringing tones sounded woefully like a challenge.

'Come, Miss Hamilton, would a mere governess disturb me?'

There was the challenge but Bryan had worked over the screenplay so long nothing but weariness entered into his voice.

'If you prefer it, I'll go inside.' Liz looked at Bryan sternly to take up his line.

The reading continued in the same vein until Alex McGovern took a deep breath and held up his hand. 'Might Miss Gilmour read the governess's part? You must be tired from your trip, Miss Stoddart, and Jane has that cool English voice, after all. The sort of voice to flutter the heart.'

'My God, you're right!' Perry's fair brows drew together in a frown. 'Hold on to that, Liz. If we're treading so carefully we need an actress who can suggest deep emotion with the smallest sigh.'

'Do you think you can make anything of it, Jane?' Liz asked kindly. 'No one expects wonders. Just do your best.'

'Give her the script,' Alex McGovern suggested.

'Here, Bryan,' Perry ordered briskly. 'I'll read for you. I was nearly going to sleep. Where are we?' he looked down. 'Ah, yes.'

'What's the matter with you, can't you sleep?' He

managed in an instant to stage a drama.

'I'm sorry, sir, did I disturb you?' When she answered after the faintest pause, Jane expelled a stifled sigh. She knew exactly how Laura Hamilton felt. There was pain in her voice, discomposure, a physical ache.

Perry looked up, glanced at her very sharply, then continued, his own reading developing until there were overtones of urgency, desperation breaking through the bright arrogance of his words.

They continued for several minutes in absolute silence so that their voices, though quiet, had a peculiar tense clarity, and the Signora, frowning in intense concentration, became more and more hunched in her chair, head down, her hands pressed hard against her quivering frame.

Finally she spoke out, startling them, and Antonella, white-faced, began to weep.

'It is good. Too good. What you say is perfectly true. This girl, of all beings in the world, could show that no evil was done. She is pure, an innocent treading a dangerous path.'

'Nonna.' Alex McGovern went to her, taking her hand and bending protectively over her fragile body.

'I'm too old for this, Sandro,' she told him.

'I'll take you up to your room, shall I?'

'*Grazie.*' She sighed her relief.

'Can't you see, Sandro, that you can't help these people?' Antonella cried emotionally, dashing tears from her glittering eyes.

'Other people will,' the old lady coughed harshly.

'Hush, Nonna.'

'It's cruel,' Antonella flared.

'Do you mind, Antonella,' Helen rose quickly and went to her mother-in-law's side. 'Alex will know what decision to make.'

'The decision is made for us, isn't it, *caro*?' The Signora leaned heavily against her grandson's arm. 'No one, *no one* can make the past go away. We can only try to show it how it was.'

It was astonishing how quickly events moved after that. Cast, crew, the teams of people necessary to make a film were brought to Monteverdi and mostly set up in the town. The town itself was ablaze with excitement—many of its people had been enlisted for various scenes—and the young girls had taken to elaborate dressing-up just in case Perry Wyndham's roving eye should suddenly fall on the one he was going to make a star. The young men stood about waiting for the delectable Carol Graham to appear and a few of the more enterprising volunteered to hold idiot boards, work in props, or offered their services as carpenters and electricians.

It was a hectic time of dawn starts and late nights, substituting lines, adding others, throwing the more contentious out. David Breeden already had his teeth into the role. The very beautiful and experienced Marina De Luca was giving some of her best work, but nothing Carol could say or do was making Perry happy.

'You're too hard on her, Perry,' Liz protested violently. 'You're always bitching about something and the poor girl loses concentration.'

'Concentration. What concentration?' Perry demanded scathingly. 'All she wants to do is bounce her bosom around. And even then there's no chemistry. And that accent! It's too damned precious. Every time I speak to her she bursts into tears.'

'He's a bully,' Liz fumed to Jane later. 'If he'd just let up on her she'd come along just fine. Of course Marina's making her look a bit wooden. Problems, problems.'

The afternoon's shooting was deplorable. Perry rebuked Carol over and over again so that she became forgetful and confused and quick-tempered. David forgot himself completely and accused Perry of being a bastard. It could have brought chaos, instead it brought laughter and some sort of order. Carol, short-sighted, wasn't much good with the cue-cards but eventually one small segment was shot perfectly.

'Jane!' Perry broke off giving instructions to one of the camermen and gestured to her to come over. 'Come for a walk with me?'

'I'm a little tired, Perry.' In fact she was exhausted.

'We'll walk slowly.' He took her arm. 'Why is it I'm a big hit in some places and with you I have to practically beg?'

'Maybe I'm trying to tell you I'm a serious person.' Perry, from the beginning, had been conspicuous with his attentions.

'And I'm not?' He lit another cigarette and inhaled deeply. Perry was a chain-smoker in an age when a lot of people had given it up, and so far as Jane could see he was a fairly heavy drinker as well, with the hospitality at Monteverdi lavish.

'I'm sorry, I don't really know you, Perry. You've been married twice.'

'Both of them wrong for me, Jane.'

'I suppose they might say the same.'

'Ouch.'

'You could be very hard to please.'

'Don't start on me about Carol. You ought to be thrilled I'm mad for you to take over her role, instead you keep protesting you've no desire to be an actress.'

'I couldn't have the responsibility of a film hanging on me. I've had no experience whatever, Perry. Surely that's important?'

Perry fetched an enormous sigh. 'Yet you're Laura

Hamilton to a T. Even McGovern thinks so. He's attracted to you, isn't he? He'd be mad if he weren't. Marina is enjoying herself no end playing up to him at dinner. Handsome devil, isn't he? And that cousin— sizzling. I could fall in love with her if I hadn't already fallen in love with you.'

'You haven't fallen in love with me, Perry,' Jane said lightly. 'Don't be absurd.'

'It's embarrassing you, I take it?' He took her arm and turned her.

'I think you enjoy falling in and out of love.' She looked up with a smile in her eyes and Perry, provoked, bent his head and kissed her.

After the initial astonishment it was pleasant but nothing Jane couldn't handle. 'Well, that got that out of the way.'

'Did you enjoy it?'

'You'll have to wait and read about it in my memoirs.'

'You're sweet, Jane, so sweet. One starts to die a little when one has no woman to love.'

Liz warned her later to take care. 'Perry's never made a movie yet that he doesn't simultaneously have a love affair. I expect it sharpens his senses. Usually it's the leading lady but God knows he's not enamoured of poor little Carol. He's giving her one hell of a time.'

'And while he's doing it he won't get any good out of her.'

'Just see he doesn't get anything out of you.' Liz sounded worried. 'The old cradle-snatcher!' She rushed away looking harassed and Jane saw Bryan grab her arm. Bryan was another one who thought Carol wasn't right for the part, but Liz for once wasn't listening. Carol was lovely to look at with plenty of experience before the cameras, so Liz was having great difficulty accepting an unknown, inexperienced, non-professional could possibly do any better. In any case, for all her tearful battles with Perry, Carol was hanging in there for all she was worth. She really wanted the part and all of them had begun to realise it was highly probable they had a winner.

When they all came together at dinner the atmosphere was fraught with little tensions, which nevertheless seemed to add sparkle to the evenings. Marina, a very elegant brunette in her mid-thirties but looking not a day over twenty-five, was having a delightful time trying to induce her host to fall into her clutches. Her progress was mostly impeded by Antonella, who in the company of men became as effervescent as champagne. The three women, Marina, Antonella and Carol, were at great pains to outshine each other in terms of glamour and seductiveness and it often seemed to Jane sandwiched between Perry and Bryan that Antonella would have had a great career on the stage. She was genuinely luscious, her accent was magic, and when she directed her great black eyes at you the adrenalin started pumping whether in fascination or fright. As Bryan put it Antonella really knew how to 'come on'.

Jane for her part was amazed Perry wasn't offering to play Svengali to Antonella instead of concentrating his persuasive powers on her, but every time they spoke together Perry could barely hold himself in check. Right or wrong he was convinced Jane could play Laura Hamilton and Jane got the impression he might stop at nothing short of murder to bring that about. Even Carol sensed the danger.

'Sometimes I think he wants to get rid of me,' she complained to Jane. The two girls had become quite friendly and Jane often acted as support and confidante. 'He would except for Liz. I can't thank you enough for working with me on my accent. Yours is so posh. I know exactly what Perry means when he tells me I'm tarted up. Accents aren't my thing.'

In fact Carol would have done quite well only Perry, of great assistance to his other lead actors, was going all out to undermine Carol's rapidly diminishing confidence. It was difficult to give a convincing performance when one was basically afraid of the director, and Perry when he chose could be quite cruel.

That particular evening after dinner Jane raced up to her room for her copy of the script so that she, Liz and Carol could run through the dialogue for the following morning's shooting. The long gallery was in darkness except for silvery fingers of moonlight that fell through the tall, arched windows in ghostly bars.

Always imaginative, Jane felt a little chill of panic. Even the back of her nape went icy. This great house had a few restless spirits and the story they were filming made the past, the house, so emotionally powerful they were all affected to varying degrees.

Carol claimed she heard voices. Liz of the forthright nature and steel nerves had told Jane in utter confidence—she didn't want anyone to think her a perfect fool—that she had sensed a presence when she was alone one night in the library. Even Bryan admitted to having been thrown off balance at different times. Of course it could easily be argued the collective mild hysteria stemmed from living the film, but there was no doubt the house had tremendous atmosphere of its own.

A thin stratum of Jane's mind was giving in. She didn't believe in ghosts, unquiet spirits or whatever, yet she made a mad dash for her door. Once she turned the light on she would be able to chide herself for surrendering to an over-active imagination, but as it was it wouldn't have surprised her in the slightest to meet Black Jack McGovern himself.

When an arm shot out of nowhere and caught her up, she screamed.

'Oh, for God's sake, shut up.'

'Alex!' It took her less than a second to realise whose arms she was in.

'Who the hell else?' he asked crisply. 'Of course it could be Wyndham, only Wyndham's downstairs.'

'You frightened me,' she breathed raggedly.

'Calm down.' He was bearing her backwards into an empty room.

'As far as that goes, how do *you* manage to be in two places at the one time?'

'Come again?'

She heard the sound of the lock as the door closed on her back. 'You *are* Alex?' she wavered. She couldn't see his face but her body knew his.

'Who do you see?' he asked sarcastically.

'Alex?' She felt totally disorientated in the dark.

'For God's sake!' His arms tightened more powerfully around her and he reached out and turned on the light. 'You sound like a jittery Victorian miss. Who were you expecting?'

'This is an old house,' she quavered. 'It could have been . . . anyone.'

He pulled back her head and kissed her mouth hard. 'Anyone? Directors, actors, extras, cameramen?'

'A lot more unmanageable than that. A lady in a crinoline, a very tall lean man with a darkly saturnine face.'

'You're joking.' He held her away from him and laughed.

'No, I'm not! We're all so involved with the filming it's enough to make anyone lose their cool. You may be used to a house on a huge scale—a house you

love—but it does have a certain atmosphere that gets
under the skin.'

'I didn't realise.' The amused mockery vanished.
'My poor little Gianina!' His hands slid over her
shoulders down her slender arms to her narrow waist.
'It seemed I would have to waylay you if I wanted to
talk to you at all. I would never wish to frighten you.'

A soft shiver ran through her that had nothing to do
with fear. Even through the crowded days when she
seemed to be at everyone's beck and call he always
occupied that closed secret place at the back of her
mind. Circumstances made it almost impossible for
her to find herself alone with him, now she realised the
deprivation to her senses. She was drinking him in,
even tilting her head back the better to see him. Over
the past weeks relationships had become so complicated she usually avoided looking overlong at him in
public. Marina, who just happened to be married, was
obviously strongly attracted to him and Antonella was
as dangerous as a loaded gun.

'You're certainly staring,' he pointed out gently, a
wry twist to his mouth. 'Have I changed in some way?'

'You're rather beautiful to look at,' she breathed,
before she could help herself.

'A man is not beautiful, *cara*.'

She opened her mouth to say something—what?—
but his hand closed under her chin, lifting her face for
his kiss. 'You've been away from me far too long.'

'They're waiting for me.'

'They won't find you.' His mouth touched hers with
exquisite restraint yet she could feel the energy that
was building up in his body, the fire.

'Alex.' She was kissing him very gently back, when
her desire for him was increasing with every second.

'There's nothing you can do.' He was working his
way around her face. Eyes, cheekbones, the whorls and

lobe of her ear, beneath her chin and now she couldn't stop bringing her arms up around his neck. To be close to him, clinging to him, was to be in sheer ecstasy, and as her will relaxed she could hear his breathing change.

His mouth stopped its gentle roaming and closed over hers, exploring it so deeply her heart was giving little gasps. Her body was flushed with heat as the blood pounded through her veins. There seemed nothing in life to rival it.

'I don't think I want to need a woman like this,' he said thickly, urgently against her cheek. 'I am hungry for everything about you.'

If their locked bodies had caught fire she would not have been surprised.

'They know I came upstairs, Alex,' she said helplessly.

'Forget them.' His hand curved in possession over the high tilt of her breast. 'Every small matter you seem to have to straighten out. Liz works you too hard. Head down typing all the time. Non-stop running—you have lost weight. Appeasing this one and that. Wyndham forever forcing himself on you. Just how long do you think I'm going to tolerate that? Now Carol. Why should you play drama coach? Why is Liz persisting in her stand? You could work on Carol forever and she would never be Laura Hamilton. She can't even begin to distill the essence of the role. A woman like that, the best and the worst kind of woman.'

She was wearing a silky evening sweater with a lurex thread and he slid his warm hands beneath it searching for her breasts.

'Alex!' Her desire was so great she felt if he touched her she would melt like snow.

'I will take care of you, little one.' He released the

catch on her bra and now his hands shaped her naked breasts.

'This is wrong.'

'Why?' His head came up and his blue eyes blazed down at her.

'You know the answer.' He still caressed her and despite herself she sighed voluptuously.

'Has Antonella been telling you I am going to marry her?'

'I don't talk to her.'

'It's important to me you trust me instead of being influenced by other people.'

'You make your grandmother very unhappy showing any interest in me.'

'So you know all about my grandmother, do you? Maybe she admires you. Have you thought of that?'

'I can't think of anything when you bring me so frighteningly alive.'

'I want you in my bed.'

'And once I'm there, what then?'

'I'll turn you mindless with delight.' He clasped her tightly to him. 'I hate it the way Wyndham follows you around.'

'You shouldn't mind.' She turned her shining head and burrowed it into his chest.

'He's an unhappy and deeply cynical man. He's also old enough to be your father. It would be best for him to turn his attentions to somebody else. Marina enjoys a flirtation. You are just a baby and I have a tiger inside me.'

'I know you do.' Her voice was blurred with emotion. 'I seem to remember your saying you don't want to feel the way you do about me.'

'Didn't you yourself say what is happening to us is scary?' he countered. 'I want to kiss you so hard I know I would hurt you. I want to take off your clothes and press you to me. I want to kiss every inch of your beautiful creamy skin. I want to draw on every emotion, every sensation you have in your body and finally when you lie under me I want you to cry out and beg me to make us one. That's what I feel like, little one. As though if I let go I could do something that might prove quite shattering to us both. You have never been a stranger. Not from the moment I set eyes on you. I knew you. You are like someone who left me when I was a child and came back. I even think of you as a little girl with long hair like silk and beautiful clear eyes. I mind I didn't know you then. I would like to know your father and mother. I think your mother must be beautiful. I like to hear you talk of your brothers—so warm and affectionate. You are a loving woman, Gianina. Made for love.'

Her hair that she had arranged in a soft, updated chignon now fell down her back and he grasped a wide swathe and allowed himself to kiss her again, the over-tight leash he kept on himself surrendering to a headlong passion.

She felt light, light as the wind itself. It was all so new to her, this insatiable sexual desire. She knew that tears slid from her eyes while he turned his head and gathered them into his own mouth. 'How beautiful you are!'

The ground was moving beneath her feet and as she suddenly seemed to slump he moved quickly, lifting her and carrying her back to a scroll-ended antique couch that occupied the position in front of the high imposing windows.

She lay back, her hair fanning over the gold-patterned green silk. Emotion heightened the sensitive modelling of her face and her thick dark lashes were wet.

'Don't cry, Gianina,' he said almost curtly. A pulse

throbbed in his temple and his brilliant blue eyes were flashing danger signals. 'I can't do as I want.'

She bit down on her lip hard. 'I feel as though my life is being ripped apart.'

'I don't want you to worry.' He took her hand, lightly slapping her blue-veined wrist. 'I should have you to myself, instead things are endlessly complicated with this wretched film. I never knew filming could be so frantic. Lie still for a moment.'

'It's a wonder someone isn't hammering down the door.'

'In my home?' One black eyebrow shot up and his high-mettled handsome face assumed what Liz called his 'Borgia look'.

'How long have we been here?'

'Don't you know?' He lifted her hand and kissed it, his vivid blue glance softening over her face.

'Ten minutes?' Eternity?

'Surely at night you should be able to relax? Liz is making a mistake persisting with Carol. She could be competent enough if Wyndham would only let up on her and she looks good but she's never going to be great. Much as I hate to agree with Wyndham on anything but I think Laura Hamilton is you.'

'A conniving little witch?' She threw his own words back at him, her green eyes abnormally large and brilliant.

'That was my defence.'

'Do you see her a little differently now?'

He turned his coal-black head abruptly. 'God knows! What is life without compassion? This film is upsetting us all.'

'I'm afraid so.' Jane felt so tired, so drained, she thought she could sleep. 'It's a story of obsession and it's so immediate. Do you suppose old houses hold on to the love and anguish and fear? Isn't it possible for a man to love two women at the same time?'

He turned back and slid his arms beneath her, the line of his jaw hardening so that he looked dangerously, darkly relentless. 'There's a vast difference between passionate love and caring. Passionate love is a lot worse than anyone could imagine. One is almost afraid of it. You are. It's quite true a man can care for two women at the same time but he loves only one. And once one loves, there is no going back.'

CHAPTER FIVE

MUCH later that night when Jane was brushing her hair for bed Liz knocked on the door.

'Got a minute, dear?'

'Sure. Come in.' Jane visibly relaxed. She had had a brief, violent brush with Antonella when she had finally returned downstairs and her nerves were over-wrought.

'Honestly you have the most beautiful hair,' Liz said admiringly and sank down in an armchair.

'Do you think so? When I was a little girl I wanted curls. My best friend, Emma, had the fattest, glossiest ringlets.'

'Like that dear girl, Antonella. Hasn't she got it in for you?'

'She doesn't care for me,' Jane agreed.

'Today has been just *hell*!' Liz passed weary hands before her eyes. 'Glorious as this place is, I'll be glad to go home. The Signora's attitude is making us all wretched. She never appears at dinner.'

'She's old,' Jane explained gently.

'Oh, I know, but if one does chance to meet her the reception is pretty ghastly. She can't wait for us to leave.'

'She is formidable.'

'A right old tartar! And Antonella! Honestly, I'd like to kick her.'

'Don't. I think she bites.'

'What was she saying to you tonight?' Liz asked worriedly.

'She was warning me off Alex.'

'I thought as much.' Liz laced her hands together as though in prayer. 'What is Alex really doing, dear girl? Please don't think I'm interfering but I'm really worried about you. God knows Alex McGovern would be dynamite to any girl, but I've had it from the Signora that an engagement between him and Antonella is all but announced.'

Jane, who had been holding on to the carved post of her Gothic bed, sank down on it abruptly. 'I think the Signora would like to see them engaged.'

'Darling,' Liz looked at her with kindly, direct eyes, 'don't overlook the old girl's influence. She might be an old dragon but Alex loves her. I wouldn't overlook the inheritance angle either. Maybe the estate is tied up. Maybe our superbly virile Alex has to toe the family line.'

Jane shook her blonde head. 'The estate passed directly to Alex. Helen told me.'

'You're in love with him, aren't you?' Liz asked with unaccustomed agitation.

'That doesn't say it,' Jane said quietly and wrapped her slender arms around her body. 'He's like a revelation. I'm a virgin, Liz.'

'Darling girl!' Liz blinked.

'I am. I've always been rather proud of my chastity. I went through the various stages of puppy love. I've been attracted to older men. I've allowed a certain amount of love-play and enjoyed it but I've never *not* been in control. I've never cared enough—nor thought anyone cared enough about me—to commit my body, my spirit, if you like. Almost from the moment I met Alex I've been a woman who is just waiting to fall into his bed. I'm madly in love with him. So madly I start trembling whenever he comes near me. I dream about him. I burn for him like a woman with a fever. I'm frightened if I'm left alone with him. I'll never get myself back at all. I'll be part of him. He'll be part of me. I'll never be a complete person alone. I love him, Liz and it's terrible.'

'And it's all his fault!' Liz wailed. 'I thought he was a man of honour, of high principles. What he's really doing is seducing you. You don't really want to tangle with that girl. Why, she's positively tigerish. I saw her tonight. She'd like to claw your eyes out.'

'She doesn't frighten me,' Jane announced. 'She upsets me but she doesn't frighten me.'

'Much good that would do you if she took it into her head to do you harm. You saw what she did to Marina? That was no accident with the lights. Marina could have sustained a nasty burn. Of course she's being a perfect fool playing up to Alex like that. I've never known Marina when she wasn't hell-bent on a flutter. But none of you are participants in a delicious game, anything and everything could happen around here. It *did*.'

Jane found it very difficult to settle after that and in the morning she felt a little ill and heavy-eyed.

'You look tired,' Perry told her quite bitterly. 'I suppose as it's rumoured, McGovern has bedded you?'

'I beg your pardon!' Jane, who had been compiling a list for Wardrobe, looked up disbelievingly.

'Right from the start he intended to have you!' Perry's tanned face looked flushed and angry. 'I can imagine the kind of fantastic time you two are having in bed.'

'Perry!' Jane threw down her pen and jumped to her feet.

'Now why look so hurt and upset?' He reached out and grabbed her wrist.

'Because I *am*. What right have you got to talk to me like this?'

'I have the right to see you don't get hurt!' A

continuity girl was approaching them and he glared at her to go away. 'I don't give a damn about McGovern. Bloody lord of creation looking down his arrogant nose. He's just playing around with you and you're letting him. I'm appalled and disgusted. I could have sworn you were a most fastidious girl.'

'Perry,' Jane's voice was low and pained, 'you do Alex a great disservice and you offend me.'

'But you're in love with him, aren't you?' he asked savagely.

'What possible difference could it make to you?'

'Just answer the question,' he ordered urgently. 'Answer.'

'I don't believe this.' With difficulty she pulled her hand away.

'I think you do.' A few people were looking at them curiously and he lowered his voice. 'We're all aware of the change in you. You might as well have it spray-painted all over you. Jane loves Alex. But are you absolutely certain he loves you?'

Jane looked up at him with helpless bewilderment. 'Why are you so angry and bitter? Why, Perry?'

'I don't like what McGovern's doing.'

'You mean the lavish hospitality he's been displaying. The food, the wine, the luxury of our accommodation. Or is it the money he's invested in the film? Perhaps it's the money.'

'He's playing around, Jane,' Perry said more quietly, the heated colour dying from his skin. 'Don't you think I did enough of it to know. You're a beautiful girl. I can understand his making a play for you but he could get you into a lot of trouble. That Antonella for all her lushness has a forbidding aspect to her nature. No one expects a jealous woman to be sweet but the looks she gives you are positively murderous.'

'Antonella is the kind of woman who has to dramatise everything.'

'She has a potential for violence,' Perry insisted. 'God, Jane, please allow me to care enough to express a warning. If McGovern hasn't ravished you already, he's going to. I see the way he looks at you. A tiger with a doe. Both of you are heading for disaster like the characters in our story. Antonella is McGovern's girl and I think she'll kill you if you get in her way.'

Jane didn't look worried. She looked disgusted. 'Surely killing people is a bit extreme. Even for Antonella.'

'She'll do her damnedest, don't you worry.' Perry thrust a shaking hand through his hair. 'Laura to the Contessa. Hasn't it struck you?'

'Except it was the *Contessa* who vanished. Please don't become agitated on my account, Perry. Allow me to handle this in my own way.'

'Sometimes I think you ought to leave.'

'I thought you wanted me to play Laura?'

'Not if you have to share McGovern's bed. Didn't poor little Laura become his mistress? He might have married her after but didn't she get a pretty rough deal? It's the Contessa who takes up the wall. The Contessa who takes pride of place. McGovern is her descendant. We've been here for weeks now but I've never seen any record of the second Mrs McGovern nor have I heard her mentioned. She was something that should never have happened. The innocent who unwittingly brought tragedy. Maybe she couldn't prevent it. You can.'

There was a powerful sincerity behind the blatant insensitivity of his words and Jane had to recognise it.

'I know you mean well, Perry,' she said gravely, 'so I'll forgive your unwarranted intrusion into my affairs.'

'You're hurting, aren't you?' he asked tersely.

'I'm well able to handle my life.'

'You can't handle McGovern. That kind of man never lets anyone stand in his way. If he wants you, he'll have you.'

'I'll have no say?' Her geen eyes were clear and slightly contemptuous.

'It's in a woman's very nature to surrender. He might be a dream lover, but believe me, sweet one, he hasn't got permanence on his mind. At least not with you. Don't let sexual fantasy trap you into tragedy. It's already caused a lot of heartbreak in his family.'

With a director so het up it was a torrid sort of day. Yet the brilliant weather held uninterrupted and outdoor shooting progressed with relatively few hassles. The schooner that was being used in the film was anchored picturesquely in the bay and most of the cast and crew liked to eat their light lunch beneath the pandanus trees that ringed the sandy crescent. Once the schooner had been a clipper-ship running opium from China to India before it had been hired to transport unwilling South Sea Islanders to the suger plantations of the north. Now it was a well preserved relic and tourist attraction and slicing a sizeable hole in the film's budget.

'Come and sit beside us,' Carol called to Jane.

'Not eating, Jane?' Marina, in costume, turned her elegant head. 'Darling, I think you're getting just the least bit too slender. You're not sickening for anything, are you?' she asked archly.

'It's too hot.' Jane sat down in an empty canvas chair. 'Where's Liz?'

'Arguing with Perry. They're not getting on at all well these days.'

'I expect it's me!' Carol bit her pretty mouth.

'Don't worry, dear, you're getting it all together,'

Marina cooed with feigned sincerity. 'And you look divine in costume.'

'You're super,' Carol announced. 'It's funny, you're anything but the snooty lady yet you play one beautifully on screen. I suppose that's what being an actress is all about.'

'Thank you, dear,' Marina drawled. 'Alex off today?' She gave Jane a gently malicious smile.

'To the island.' Jane returned the glance with cool equanimity. 'I'd love to go sometime.'

'So would I,' Marina agreed with emphasis. 'Did he take his crazy little cousin as well?'

'I think so.'

'There's a whiff of madness about that girl. I'm an Italian but I don't act like Vesuvius going up.'

'They're not ordinary, that's for sure,' Carol ventured. 'She makes me feel positively slack but Helen's so nice. She's the only one who doesn't seem obsessed with the old scandal. What do *you* think happened to the Contessa?' she asked Jane.

'I can't even begin to speculate.' Jane shook her head.

'Maybe she was on the grog,' Marina offered. 'Some women do start to drink when they're unhappy. My sister did after her divorce. Maybe our Contessa got drunk and wandered off. Maybe a crocodile took her. Bryan was telling me they used to waddle into town in the old days.'

'He was pulling your leg.' Carol looked amazed.

'No, he wasn't.' Marina shook her elaborately dressed head. 'He said planters used to sit up on their verandahs and shoot them as they went past.'

'What a diversion!' Jane shuddered.

'The big fellas, the old estuarine variety can live up to three hundred years and more.'

'Small wonder they look like that,' Jane said wryly and began to fan herself.

'Maybe if the crocodile is still around he could tell us,' Carol stammered, round-eyed. 'It's all so terribly spooky. Perry is really getting it into the film. A woman vanishes without trace. I've been having nightmares since I arrived. Then I wake up suddenly and I'm positive it was to voices.'

'Spare us, darling,' Marina drawled. 'Could be you're going too heavy on the vino. Have you ever seen anyone fuss so much setting a scene up?' She looked back towards the terrace where Perry and the crew were working. 'Don't try too hard this afternoon, ducky,' she advised Carol. 'Remember I am the great plantation-owner's wife. You are just the little governess. Restraint is everything . . . lowered eyes.'

As a piece of advice it fell on deaf ears. For the first five takes Carol played the part with a kind of irrepressible pert insolence of which she seemed totally unaware.

'Can you do anything I ask you?' Perry demanded. He held up his hand demanding perfect quiet and a few moments later called, 'Action.'

Insolence became a faint retardation and Perry began to bully her unmercifully. He was coaxing a superb performance out of Marina but Carol's whole style was maddening him so much at last he yelled furiously he was fit to be locked up.

'It's the dregs!' Carol wailed and burst into tears. 'Perry just doesn't know how to appreciate me.'

That was all too apparent.

'Poor little thing, she'll have to go!' Liz mourned. 'It's lousy. I cast her, but there you are. Basically I suppose she *is* second-lead material. Bryan is always telling me. I thought her looks might carry the day but even her looks have been a surprise. She's too saucy. A man would be more likely to pinch her than lust after her in private. That's been troubling me as much as the performance. Of course Perry has worked up an unhealthy hate. Poor girl, she'll be devastated and I suppose he'll ask me to deliver the *coup de grâce.*'

In the end something far more terrifying happened.

Dinner was a queer mock-up of the day's frustrations. Alex had come back from the island in a kind of devilish, challenging mood that became more pronounced as Jane tried to withdraw. Too many forces were pressing down on her tonight, a retreat from all the whirling excitement.

Surprisingly Antonella too was quiet and Jane guessed that she and Alex might have had an argument. There was a kind of grief in the depths of her black eyes and she scarcely noticed the way Marina responded to her cousin's disturbing mood, throwing her head back and laughing almost wildly. Marina was finding a change of mood exciting and as Jane glanced briefly in Alex's direction she was more than ever aware he would move most women. A kind of glitter was on him, a patina of light. Hair, skin, eyes shone. When he smiled, his teeth were a white flash against his darkly tanned olive skin. He looked for all the world like an impossibly handsome buccaneer, brilliant-eyed and mocking and underneath, ruthless.

Immediately dinner was over he walked around to Jane's chair and held it. 'You can spare Jane tonight, can't you, Liz? She looks pale.'

'We're shooting the banquet scene in the morning,' Perry pointed out pleasantly, though his eyes were cold.

'Then I must watch it,' Alex responded smoothly, a hint of male aggression in his sparkling blue eyes. 'I'm told processed film has been flown back and it's excellent.'

'The talent, so-so,' Perry said in frustration.

'Backdrops superb. As a location Monteverdi could scarcely be bettered. If you'd care to see the rushes now we'll set them up.'

'I'm looking forward to seeing them,' Alex assured him suavely. 'Could you possibly allow us fifteen minutes or so? Jane is all eyes. A walk in the fresh air will do her good.'

'Pompous ass!' he said to Jane when they were well out of earshot. 'He eats my food. He drinks my wine. How does he work and drink so much? He is shattered you see anything in me at all. I'm sure he has even told you to beware.'

'And why not? You're a very dangerous man.'

'If you mean I'm going to kiss you, devour you, you're right.' He took her arm, leading her down the banks of exotic plants and water gardens. 'Next time I go to the island, you're coming with me. Much has been accomplished in a remarkably short time.'

'It's a big project, isn't it?'

'Millions of dollars will go into it. I can't bear not to show it to you.'

'Nothing went wrong, did it?' she asked shakily. 'I thought the family were ... subdued.'

'Perhaps a little.' He was abruptly his imperious self. 'Toni put on one of her tantrums. She has been very badly brought up.'

'I thought she looked almost tragic at dinner. I suppose when you wanted to be you could be rather cruel.'

His eyes slid over her averted face and slender figure. 'Aren't you jumping to harsh conclusions? I have never been cruel to Antonella. Or any other woman. A man is not a man when he makes a woman suffer.'

'I expect they suffer all the same.'

'What is this, Gianina?' He turned her to him. 'Why

do you allow Antonella to affect you so? So she is jealous of you? I can't deny it. She has always regarded me as her own. Even as a little girl she was like that. It's not something new. We've all spoilt her, indulged her and now it's become tiresome. Toni cannot be allowed to dictate any aspect of my life. I was not cruel—I could not be that—but I was firm enough to get through to her.'

'Poor Antonella!'

He saw her face tauten. 'Surely we can find something better to talk about? She has treated you abominably, now you feel sorry for her.'

'But you made love to her. Alex.'

'I've made love to a lot of women,' he said crisply. 'Does this mean I'm a scoundrel, a heartless seducer? I want *you*.'

Though she meant to arch away from him she found her body yielding. A fruit-bat winged low overhead and she dipped her head against him.

'I've missed you so much. All day.' His hands were roving, caressing her body. 'Perhaps my worst sin is wanting you.'

She kept silent for a moment, listening to the thud of his heart, and he lifted her head and began to kiss her with a tenderness that just concealed a rising passion.

'You said you wanted to come with me to the rain-forest. Just when do these people give you time off?'

'It will be a full day tomorrow.' She turned her head so he was murmuring a little fiercely in her ear.

'Dammit, Jane. Come with me.'

'I desperately want to.'

He bent his head and kissed the soft hollow in her throat. 'I'll kidnap you if you don't. It's a wonderful green world. A unique world. Trees are in flower. Many in fruit. The forest is filled with birdsong.

Orchids flourish in the forks of trees, marvellous hanging gardens of mosses and ferns and on the edge of the rain-forest, the butterflies. Such butterflies, with wings as velvety as your throat.'

'It sounds marvellous.'

'Then you'll come?'

'I can't. I must be on hand, Alex. That's my job.'

'Then it's a terrible job! You're much thinner than you were. It occurs to me they don't pay you properly for all the long hours and your eyes are too big in your face. When I came in tonight it seemed to me you were exhausted. I wanted to pick you up and cradle you in my arms, instead you retreated as though you were afraid of me. Sometimes I think it's even true. Are you afraid of me, Jane?'

How could she explain that sometimes she felt an overpowering sense of dread as though something terrible was about to happen? People did experience premonitions. She was sick, suffocating with love for him. When he kissed her, held her, she felt violent excitement. She thought when she fell in love it would be peaceful and steady, a quiet flame.

'Gianina?' He turned up her face to him. Perhaps it was a trick of the moon but his face was subtly different: older, tauter, harder, the eyes not blue but dark.

Her heart was pumping wildly. 'Who are you really?' she asked.

'I think you're very much overtired.'

'It's been a long day,' she said a little vaguely. 'I am tired. I haven't been sleeping well.'

'You want me beside you, that's why.' He slanted a frowning glance over her silvery-fair head. 'If it would help you sleep I would sit in a chair and watch over you. It would give me pleasure to hear your quiet breathing. To know you were getting the rest you needed. As it is, I can feel your heart racing under my hand.'

They were standing in the shadow of the tall Italian cypress when a shower of small white marble chips came cascading down the steps.

'Alex! Alex!' It was Helen, shouting, waving. It was a cry of extreme agitation.

'God!' He pulled back though he still kept an arm around Jane. 'It must be Nonna.'

'Go to her quickly.' In a moment Jane had thrown off her deadly lethargy.

'Come here, come with me.' He grasped her hand and pulled her swiftly after him until they were standing on the upper terrace listening to Helen. 'It's Carol. She's unconscious.' Helen, usually so composed and confident, looked distraught. 'One minute she was talking to me, the next she seemed to have a little seizure. We'll have to get her to hospital.'

The blood drained rapidly out of Alex's handsome face. 'Tell Gino to get the car out.'

'It's out.'

They were moving rapidly into the entrance hall. 'Where is she?'

'The atrium. Perry is trying to revive her. I've never seen anything so . . . Oh, Alex!'

Carol was still lying on the floor looking appallingly waxy and fragile.

'We know what it was.' Robert McGovern had his strong hands crushed together, gazing down at the stricken girl. 'Red-back. Liz saw it retreating into a corner and I killed it.'

'A red-back in the house?' Alex dropped to his knees and got his arms around the unconscious girl. 'How would a red-back get into the house?'

Jane felt so sick she thought she would faint. 'What is a red-back?'

'A spider, dear. A deadly spider.' Helen took one look at Jane's face and pressed her down into a chair.

'Oh, Alex, what is going to happen?' Like Liz, the tears were starting to Jane's eyes. 'She's not going to die?'

'I'm getting her to hospital right now. Telephone ahead, Helen,' he said urgently. 'There's anti-venom. You're sure it was a red-back, Robert?'

'No doubt.' Robert McGovern nodded his head sombrely. 'Yellow stripe right down the back. How it got into the house I'll never know, let alone into Jane's shawl. Spiders don't go searching for people. They hide.'

Alex gathered Carol's slight unconscious body higher in his arms. 'The spider was in Jane's shawl?'

Jane's stomach was as tight as a knot. 'I'll come with you, Alex.'

'Me too.' Liz took a moment off to dab at her eyes. 'I feel so responsible. I was the one who suggested a walk. Poor little Carol reached out and put the shawl around her shoulders. Both she and Jane have that white skin insects like to bite. Oh, God!' she choked off.

Alex didn't argue with them. He turned about and strode quickly to the courtyard where the chauffeur had the car waiting.

'It's all right, I'll drive.' Alex put Carol into the back seat of the car and Liz moved in on the other side cradling Carol's pale, clammy face in her lap.

It was a nightmare trip to the hospital, breaking all speed limits.

'People die from these spider bites, don't they, Alex?' Liz asked once.

'She won't die.' Alex's face was grim and austere.

'We're going to get her to the hospital where she's going to be treated.'

'It should have been me,' Jane said.

'Don't think about it now,' Alex warned.

'Had we been in the atrium I would have picked it up. I left it there last night. Are spiders attracted to the orchids?'

'No.' Alex answered in no uncertain fashion. 'First we'll look after Carol, then we'll try and discover how the red-back got there. They usually like dark, secret places, not a place full of sound and light. Though anything is possible, I suppose.'

It was a long sleepless night but by early morning they had the wonderful news that Carol had responded well to treatment.

'She's out of danger,' Alex rang. He had remained all night at the hospital at his own insistence but the two women had been sent home.

'Isn't that the most wonderful news!' Helen had taken the message and woken Jane up to tell her.

'It's the most wonderful news I've ever heard in my life,' Jane said feelingly. 'You could say the whole thing was meant for me.'

'I know how you feel, dear.' Helen leaned forward and patted her hand. 'It's our home and it should never have happened. Alex was dreadfully upset. One feels so responsible. But anyway, God's good, and no real harm has come to her. She might be a bit groggy for a day or two but Alex said she came out of it well. The young are resilient.'

The only person who wasn't elated was Antonella. She was descending the stairway as Jane was coming back in from the sunlight.

'Good morning.' With Carol out of danger Jane was in a mood to be kind and forgiving. Even to Antonella.

Antonella did not speak or smile. She continued on her way in a peculiarly lifeless fashion, for once not her usual glossy self but rather careless and sallow.

'Are you all right, Antonella?' Jane asked instinctively. She was appalled by the other girl's uncharacteristic appearance, and believed that Antonella, like the rest of the family, held herself responsible for the safety of their guests.

Antonella's head snapped up and for the first time she acknowledged Jane's presence,

'It's your fault, you know that?'

'Are you okay?' Jane persisted.

'I've seen through you right from the beginning.'

'What do you mean?' Jane couldn't ignore the battery of jealous hostility any more.

'Why don't you go home?'

Jane shrugged. 'I will be going home when the filming is over. There's a lot more to be done at our studios in Sydney.'

'It would be worth almost anything to get rid of you.'

'Why?' If what Alex was saying was true, Antonella couldn't be allowed to cling to the idea *she* was the important person in his life.

'You think I would let you have my one dream in life?'

'It would be much better for you to face up to reality than dream, Antonella,' Jane said quietly.

Antonella's burning black eyes became queerly unfocused. 'How can you trust him?'

'I do.'

'Men are deceivers. All of them. I'm telling you the truth.'

'Do you love Alex?' Jane stopped at the bottom of the stairs and looked up at the other girl.

'Love, what's that?' Antonella shrugged her slim

shoulders. 'I have been part of Sandro all my life. Nonna has always told me one day I would marry him. She has told me this from a little girl.'

'Yet you've had other affairs, Antonella, isn't that true?' Jane was determined to get to the bottom of it. 'Young men in your own country madly in love with you. You're a beautiful girl.'

'Not one of them would stand up to Sandro,' Antonella flashed contemptuously. 'Not one I couldn't drop in a week.'

'But you've allowed them to make love to you?'

For a second Antonella looked almost confounded, then her brow cleared. 'So?' She shrugged her shoulders. 'Is there any reason why I should deny myself passing pleasure? I am a woman. Men admire me. I want them to admire me. It is important for a woman. But this has nothing to do with my separate world. It is a kind of ... appetite. You will understand. Sandro is *mine*. He is the only human being I have ever truly loved. The only man I have ever wanted.'

'But he must want *you*, Antonella, don't you see?'

'He *does* want me. He *loves* me.'

'But surely not enough to make you his wife?'

Antonella looked at Jane as though she hadn't understood a word she said. 'You are the one who is causing all this unhappiness. You are nothing to Sandro but an easy conquest. I was very wrong, I admit ...' She broke off suddenly and drew back in confusion.

'Wrong about what?'

Someone else stepped in. A torrent of Italian issued from the top of the stairs and as both girls looked up Alex's grandmother hit the floor with her cane.

'Antonella, be quiet!' she sounded shockingly harsh.

'Please talk to her, Nonna.' Antonella started to run

back up the stairs. 'She thinks I will let her have my one dream in life.'

'Let me help you, Signora.' Jane started forward as the old lady seemed to sway.

'Leave me.' Jane was waved off. 'You should not have come down, Antonella. I told you to stay where you were.'

'I couldn't help it!' Antonella cried explosively. I had such nightmares. The tablets you gave me, they did nothing. Nothing.'

'You will please return to your room now,' the Signora ordered. 'You must do as I say.'

'Yes, Nonna.' Astonishingly Antonella answered like a spent little girl.

'Plans, good or bad, what does it matter?' the old lady shrugged. 'Life takes us and throws us around like clay. I can stop nothing. I never could.'

CHAPTER SIX

IT was Carol herself who decided she had had enough of Monteverdi and afterwards an unrepentant Perry—now that Carol was better—came to Jane and put his arm around her shoulder. 'You're going to do this, Janey,' he told her. 'And they'll always remember *I* gave you your first chance.'

For once it was a case of an unwilling understudy pushed into the main role. Heady as the honour was and in her good moments Jane found it irresistible, she had the undermining feeling her complete lack of training would show. She simply wasn't a professional and she had always found amateurs rather awful. Playing Juliet in her final school year (admittedly to the best possible audience) had given her a taste for acting but it seemed dreadfully clear to her the story hinged on Laura.

'You aren't the first novice to carry off a star part,' Liz consoled her. 'When he's not stinkin', Perry is a brilliant director. Just put yourself in his hands.'

Perry, given his way in all things, and delighted to have Carol removed, turned overnight from a monster to the most supportive and considerate of mentors. Long shots could be saved. Jane and Carol were of similar height, weight and colouring. Jane already knew all Laura's dialogue. Her accent was perfect and test shots confirmed the camera loved her, and what was even more important she appeared entirely natural before it. She *was* Laura Hamilton whether she liked it or not.

Rehearsed the night before, scenes were reshot with

astonishingly few takes. 'Extraordinary' was a word that was used often. Jane thought it was because she identified so readily with the character she was playing. A real woman, no movie invention. Also, given the quality of the combined performances, Brian was coming up with even better lines and the further effect of starting on another novel at the same time.

'Please make it total fiction, darling,' Liz warned.

The important banquet scene that they all had been dreading was shot after the third take with never one slip from the principal players. Indeed the people who worked hardest were the make-up girls effecting running repairs under the hot, brilliant lights. Laura, as the governess, had no lines at all but much was required in the way of changing expressions in her eyes. She had to forget herself entirely. She was a brave and intelligent young woman set adrift in an alien landscape. She was pure of heart, intensely loyal to her employers and utterly horrified to find herself drawn magnetically to a legendary man; a man, moreover, who was held to worship his beautiful but obviously unhappy wife.

'Darling, this is the perfect vehicle for you!' Perry cried. 'Could anything touch those eyes!'

Jane only knew she had to blink those eyes rapidly to bring herself back to reality. She understood now how actors became so immersed in a role they found it difficult to switch off. The truly astounding thing was that David Breeden, her leading man, began to develop a romantic interest in her which perversely Perry encouraged for the 'chemistry' but which was starting to upset David's current girlfriend, who shared a secluded bungalow with him on the outskirts of the town.

'Don't worry about it,' Liz advised Jane. 'Most leading men find it useful to fall in love with their leading ladies at least as long as the filming lasts. Perry, wicked old thing, is only experimenting. You ought to speak to Susan so that she understands. I know he's handsome and rugged and all that but there's nothing underneath. He's so vain!'

It was dreamlike, dramatic. It was also very hard work. 'I think Jane had better have the day off tomorrow,' Alex insisted. 'One of the wardrobe girls was telling me they're forever altering her costumes.'

'Why not?' Things were going so well Perry was operating on a high. 'We have plenty to keep us going. I've been thinking a great deal about that mob scene.'

In fact relations between Jane and Alex had become very strained; partly because she had speculated on Antonella's odd behaviour at the time of Carol's shock trauma and Alex had become very severely 'family', and partly because they were suffering frustrations of the worst kind. Filming was such an obsessive occupation the affairs of real life almost had to be repressed. Jane who was essentially a very well balanced person found herself weeping a lot if only in the privacy of her room, and she thought this had a good deal to do with being overworked. Miscasting had held them up and precious time had to be made up. The truly wondrous thing was that Perry, who drank like a fish, had more energy than all of them, even if Jane was sure it would all, inevitably, catch up with him. His interest in her these days had taken on a quite different quality. He never once attempted to kiss her, when David tried all the time, but rather enjoyed the traditional Svengali-Trilby roles. For the time of the filming, Jane was his 'thing', his creation. He had discovered her all by himself and there was every reason to suppose she would continue his protégée if she wanted a career.

'I had no idea you were so wonderfully talented,'

Liz said. 'Perry is already saying you'll be able to pick and choose.'

Did none of them realise Jane was totally unmoved by the thought of a successful acting career? For one thing it was hard work with little time for relaxation and of necessity actors nourished a very healthy ego to help them handle so much criticism. Jane, a genuine beauty, had little vanity when great battles had gone on between Marina and Carol to draw the greatest admiration. Even David and Marina often became hot and bothered about seemingly trivial things such as the power of certain camera angles and the advisability of being photographed more from the left than the right. Marina fretted endlessly about the slight sharpness of her aristocratic nose and David refused point-blank to surrender up even one of his lines. At the times when they watched their own technicolour images on a screen Jane thought she couldn't possibly be as 'affecting' as she appeared—there was something quite lovely about the blonde young woman there on the screen—but Marina often groaned aloud at her looks more than her performance.

'I loathe my nose. I've always loathed my nose. It's so sharp and bony.'

'Forget your nose,' Bryan told her. 'Your nose is okay.'

It seemed ludicrous to talk about noses when there was so much urgent drama going on. Marina was a superb Contessa, the living embodiment of a beautiful, ultra-civilised young woman living in a dark, de-structive jungle. Yet for all that, Jane's cool, lily-like presence held sway. She was tremendously effective as the innocent victim desperately trying to exorcise passion.

After all, it was real life.

'I wish to God it were all over,' Alex told her. 'As

far as I'm concerned making films is to be in a perpetual state of chaos and unreality. I can understand why Breeden's girlfriend isn't talking to him. He's obviously decided falling in love with you will contribute to an Academy Award performance.'

'So what time are we leaving?' Jane asked him.

'I really should let you sleep in.' His blue eyes were fixed on her pale face.

'Please don't! I'm in one of the most beautiful parts of the world and I can't seem to see anything. I'm longing to see the rain-forest.'

He slanted over her a disturbing glance. 'Even with me? I thought you'd undergone some massive surgery to your heart.'

'You know we've got problems, Alex.' She sat back in her rattan chair looking up at the night. 'You hold it against me for implying Antonella could have had something to do with what happened to Carol.'

'And I told you why,' he answered curtly. 'I mean, had she, it would have been criminal. Toni is a number of things but I know she would stop short of——'

'Trying to drive people away? That's the kindest interpretation. What happened was meant for me.'

His chiselled mouth thinned. 'This filming has made such a sick idea take root in your mind. I have spoken to Toni. I have spoken to everyone. I did everything in my power to compensate Carol.'

'You were very generous to her.'

'She had undergone a distressing experience in my house. I've considered this over and over. My anger and fear was far greater as you might easily have been the victim, but don't ask me to blame my poor cousin.'

'I didn't ask you to blame her.' Jane twisted up. 'I asked you to check.'

'I did check.' He caught her slender shoulders

beneath his hands. 'I check every minute of the day. In my anxiety when I'm not here Gino watches over you with great care.'

'I know you arranged for Gino to act as my bodyguard.'

'This is idiotic, our fighting.'

'I don't want to fight, Alex,' she said carefully. 'But I can't help feeling something is very wrong with Antonella.'

'You want me to send her home?'

'I'd feel better, but I have no right to ask such a thing. Antonella has been part of you all her life. I understand what you're feeling, Alex. It's just I suppose I'm hurt, disappointed you would think I suggested Antonella out of malice. What happened was dreadful and Antonella's behaviour the next day was very odd. She was aggressive and nervous. Your grandmother certainly didn't want her to talk.'

'Please, stop, Jane, please.'

'I'm sorry.' She lowered her head. 'I know how much you love them.'

'Do you know what I feel about you?' His words weren't in the least lover-like but rather cruelly intent.

'Whatever it is, I can't stand it!' She reacted emotionally to his faint violence.

'I can see that.'

'Let me go, Alex.' She tilted up her chin.

'Yes, go to bed, little girl.'

'I expect we should forget our trip?'

'I wouldn't try to put it off if I were you.' Something very turbulent prowled in his eyes.

A little swallow rippled her throat. 'Then what time?'

His glance sharpened and a biting, sardonic note entered his voice. 'I would try to get as much sleep as I could. Dawn would be the best time to leave.'

*　　*　　*

They walked for a long time before either of them said a word.

It was a warm, humid, green world that here and there was brilliantly lit as the sun pierced through the heavy crown of the trees. Jewel-coloured birds stripped blossoms of their nectar. Jane had never been in such a forest before. This was full tropical rain-forest where the plant life was overwhelming. Every inch of a tree—trunk, branches, even leaves—was covered with trailing growths of mosses, lichens and beautiful filmy ferns. There were great thick woody vines hanging down from the treetops like gigantic ropes, or twining around tree trunks in strangling loops.

The vines to Jane's eyes gave the forest its distinctive appearance. Some even looked unsupported like some magical Indian rope trick. Orchids cascaded from the trees in abundance. There were other epiphytes too: staghorns and elkhorns, spectacular giants, and the curious phenomenon known as cauliflory where large bunches of white flowers grew from a few inches above the ground to forty or fifty feet up the magnificent rain-forest giants. In the rather eerie green gloom the trees stood out like beacons brightening the overpowering effect of the vines and the fig-trees and the glorious tree ferns.

Alex went slightly ahead of her, clearing and checking, a lean, powerful figure in fitted jeans and a khaki bush-shirt. He seemed very much preoccupied with his own thoughts but once when Jane went to examine a strongly scented flower that had taken root in a dead fallen branch, he pulled her away abruptly.

'Don't touch anything without checking with me first.'

'Even you?'

'Especially me.'

'I see,' she said quietly. In the enshrouding green light her own beauty was ethereal. Her silvery fair hair drawn back by a green scarf trailed down her back and her wonderfully expressive eyes were darkened to jade.

'I don't know that you do.' He looked down at her rather sombrely, then moved on.

Some people plodded, Jane thought, head down, almost mechanical. He moved soundlessly with the rhythm and controlled grace of a sleek jungle cat. Some time she would have to talk to him but she would have to wait until he was in a more receptive mood. It was terrible what she had implied but inside she was in a sort of rage with what might have happened. Her instincts never let her down and she was certain Antonella knew far more than she was saying. What it really came down to was blood was much thicker than water. Once she had gone Monteverdi would go back to its old ways.

'Alex, I'm going to have to take a rest soon!'

The sound of her voice through the glimmering green corridors caused a disturbance to the birds. They darted from tree to tree, calling to each other; scarlet, gold, enamelled green and a superb turquoise blue. There were legions of birds, now highly vocal.

'It couldn't have been very different in the Garden of Eden!' She laughed and put up her hands. Swirls of leaves and pink and scarlet blossom were descending like a perfumed mist alighting on her hair and on her shoulders like bright butterflies.

'We'll rest here for a few moments,' Alex told her, turning away abruptly and walking to a forest giant whose massive buttresses towered twenty feet or more, forming a circle of shallow wooded caves.

'This is exquisitely beautiful!' Jane exclaimed. 'It's like the beginning of the world when everything was fresh and green.'

'There was trouble even in Eden,' he said briefly.

'How long is it before we reach the pool?' She sank gracefully beside him.

'Maybe half an hour. We'll swim first, then we'll have something to eat. You can swim nude if you like.'

'I have my swimsuit on underneath.'

'Relax,' he said. 'I know.' His blue eyes fell to the shadowed cleft of her breast. A little of her bikini top was showing through the thin pink cotton of her shirt.

The pool when they came to it was glorious. It was fed by a stream that coursed down the mountain so that streaming white cascades dashed over the encircling rocks and trailed silver ribbons across water so deeply green it was like polished jet in the shadows.

'May I go in?' she asked him a little tauntingly.

'No one in this wide world is going to stop you.'

'Thank you.' She bowed her head ironically, but her body was so heated and the pool looked so cool she pulled off her shirt and her jeans without another word. Her body had the same particular beauty as her face but she wasn't even aware of herself, nor of the sudden fire in his eyes.

She stood at the edge like a dancer, fashioning her hair into a high plait and catching it under with a gold clip. 'If Perry had known about this, he would have tried to fit it into the film.'

'There have to be some parts of the earth left as they were at the beginning.' He leaned back on a rock with exquisite ease. 'Dive in. I'm warning you, it will be cold.'

'As good as done!' She moved out on to a boulder, then entered the water smoothly, going down, down into the lustrous green depths then rising to laugh into the sun. 'Beautiful! Could anything be more beautiful?'

He seemed to enjoy watching her. Perhaps it was softening his mood? Then after a while he stripped off his own clothes and stood tall and taut like a bronze statue, black briefs his only garment. His bare feet moved over the ground with ease and a second later he was in the water beneath her, grasping her around the waist and lifting her out of the water with an effortless display of muscular power.

She was coming down in slow motion, her face poised above him, her body as weak as if he were making violent love to her. He was deliberately tormenting her. It was just his kind of thing and Jane tried desperately to still her leaping senses.

It was a queer kind of water-ballet where they seemed to be testing each other to the limit. He knows how much I ache for him, Jane thought. She skimmed across the green surface, trod water beneath the rushing cascades and when she took a breath it was like a shudder.

When he came near her, she twisted sharply and swam away. When she was far enough she began to float. It was like magic in the water. They were both accomplished swimmers but the ripples at her centre were making further exertion almost painful. Sooner or later she would have to come out. To lie beside him on a rock. To be enveloped by his aura.

He was the first one to pull himself out of the water. He stood on a boulder, reaching down a hand to her. His dark golden body was haloed in the greenish-gold light. She had never seen a man so perfectly made, his potent masculinity a tangible force.

'Come, Gianina,' he ordered. 'You've had enough.' He pulled her up on to the rock before him, their wet, glistening bodies coming into electric contact and irresistibly fusing.

There was no stopping her reaction. She moaned.

'What is it, *cara*?' He taunted her gently, grasping her darkened, plaited hair and watching her face.

Her body was quivering like the strings of a bow, pressing into his as her most basic, powerful instincts were overcoming the commands of the mind.

'Kiss me,' she begged him between a whisper and a wail.

'You sound desperate.' Something hurting within him made her curb her wild impatience.

'I am. Can't you see it in my eyes?' Indeed her beautiful eyes showed only the image of himself.

'And after I've kissed you, what then?' A hard, almost ruthless expression crossed his dark face. 'Are you ready for a lover or do you want to remain an innocent girl?'

'Alex.' The sun caught in her emerald eyes.

'Do you think you can play with me? Let your body tremble against mine? Do you think you can beg me to kiss you and when you change me into a madman you can beg me to stop? I want you desperately, Gianina. If I kiss you now, in this place, I won't be able to stop.'

'The way you couldn't stop with Antonella?' Inexplicably she was rocked by a violent anger. Her desire for him was so uncontrollable she had to shatter it somehow.

'Don't say any more. Not a word.' His lean, powerful body was perfectly rigid as though he were trying to hold on to what control he had.

'What's happening to me. What's happening to me?' she said despairingly, beginning to turn aside. 'All my life I've felt calm and secure, now you've drawn me through the doorway of another world.'

'You are quite the little coward,' he said cuttingly.

'Am I?' She was shaking though the hot sun was warming and drying her body.

'Hasn't it occurred to you before?'

'Because I'm totally unprepared for loving you?'

'Ah, you've said it.' His vibrant voice had a fine, goading edge. 'Aren't you ashamed?'

'Alex, why are you so cruel to me?' Her slender body arched over as she felt a throb of pain.

'You don't seem to appreciate you've got me nearly out of my mind. Why don't I say to you—what right have you to turn my life upside down? I was quite happy before. There was none of this terrible urgency for a woman. There have been other beautiful girls in my life. I don't care to speak of one woman to another—even you—but I felt you had to know about Antonella. What happened between us seemed light-years ago. I regret it. I would undo it if it were at all possible. Why do you keep throwing Antonella at me?'

'Because she loves you,' Jane shouted, her own love making her small breasts heave. 'She loves you. She'll get you—by *any* means and she has your grandmother's powerful support.'

'So that settles it, does it?' He took one step towards her. 'I allow my life to be run by women? My God, dismiss the thought. How was this Women's Lib ever allowed? A woman is not equal to a man. She never was and she never will be. She might be beautiful, bright, intelligent. She might be the light of his life but she does not dictate to him at any time.'

'That's right,' she cried. 'Turn on the Italian. Even your accent changes.'

'You are aware that you are my woman.'

'Alex.' He was advancing on her and she couldn't raise a hand against him. Her voice was ragged with fright. Who could argue equality when confronted by a powerful, angry man? Her naked flesh was scorched by the heat that emanated from his body.

'Yes?' His brilliant, blue eyes stared down at her, the resonant tone slightly slurred.

'You did warn me you had a tiger in you,' she said helplessly.

'So?' He remained towering over her. 'However angry you make me I don't think I could ever hurt you. You would be surprised how frightened men are of a woman's fragility. They would like to beat her, but they can't, so they kiss her instead.'

She looked up at him with such a strange and vulnerable expression he groaned aloud. 'You're perfect. Perfect. I'm terrified of you.'

Her eyelids were so weighted they fell. Even her bones melted as he reached for her, her heart leaping excitedly in her virgin's breast.

'I'll be very gentle with you, Gianina.'

Ribbons of birds flew across the sun.

He lifted her high in his arms and bore her down into the thickly carpeted soft ground, his mouth covering hers very slowly as though sensitive to her defencelessness.

It pierced her to the very heart.

His voice had lost all its usual sardonic crispness. He was murmuring to her, words she knew, the more intriguing Italian. He was treating her very gently as though their passion could never match.

When his fingertips ringed her nipples it was like circles of blue fire. 'You like that, don't you?' he asked.

In truth her heart was pounding as if it were about to burst.

'It seems so natural for me to take you here. I have always loved this spot. It still has the magic of childhood. Do you understand?'

The sensations he was arousing were so powerful she only vaguely heard him. She was intensely within his power, her hands fluttering by her side, palms up like a supplicant's.

'You're all right, Gianina?' He brushed his mouth back and forth over her own.

She gave a little convulsive sigh.

'There is so much I want to do to you. So much you know nothing of.' He put his mouth to her breast and her hips arched, almost sprang, off the ground.

'Little one. *Carissima.*' His voice was drugged with sensuality. 'You don't want me to stop, do you?'

'No.'

Soft as it was he heard her.

He slid his hands down over her body and his touch was sublime. Air rippled over her naked body, touched it, teased it, while his caressing fingers electrified her skin.

'Your skin is like cream.'

Her eyes shut even tighter so that she could absorb this exquisite rapture. It consumed her like a bath of fire. A few times in her life she had questioned her own celibacy but the explanation was here. She was giving her body to the man she loved. It had been strictly reserved and now she was fiercely glad.

His hands were moving rhythmically, savouring her satiny skin, setting up little spasms. Each movement, each spiral brought a fresh sensation, a fresh quiver, a craving for more. He was concentrating entirely on her, awakening her passions with a consummate artistry so that her body couldn't contain them and her slender legs began to move restlessly.

'Alex.'

'Yes?' He lifted his raven head.

'Help me.'

He understood, just as he knew how to prolong the burning torment. 'I will help you, Gianina. Soon. *Soon.* I want you to remember this all your life.' He lowered his mouth to the slight, taut curve of her belly, his tongue tracing the little carved depression, moving slowly downwards.

'Darling.' Her heart was fluttering in her breast and she sank her fingers into his thick, curling hair.

Now at last he was where he wanted to be and she could stand no more. Her hands moved convulsively and her almond nails grazed his back. 'Alex, I want you. Need you. Please.'

His powerful body responded instantly, whip-cord hard and arching into urgency. His expression was almost one of a man in agony so stripped was it of all veneer. Stripped and raw with sensitivity. The fire that consumed him, consumed her.

As he moved deeply into her body she gave a long, tremulous sob, but as he half lifted himself away from her she imprisoned him with her slender legs. She was a flash away from a bone-shattering, flesh-melting climax and she would allow nothing to hold back those deep tumultuous currents.

When he found her so ready, fire poured out of him, a heat of such intensity, flesh felt like seared silk.

Her mouth sought his frantically and her slender limbs coiled him round. She was in some other dimension now, filled up with love, rapture and a firestorm of abandonment.

'Now!' he cried gaspingly, holding her floating face up to him, and on an infinitely fine edge she responded to his signal, locking his body to hers with strong, silken inner muscles so that he shuddered in a kind of unending exultation and roared to a climax.

It was too much for her. Mind and body slipped earthly confines and went soaring after her soul.

For a long time afterwards she lay utterly quiet in his arms while he stroked her skin very gently much as one would a baby. He had caused her tremendous

excitation, now he wished to soothe her before he
brought her to another brink. When he led her down
to the water she plunged in. It was like liquid
diamonds and they were as naked and pure as the first
man and woman in Paradise.

When he took her for the second time it was heart-
stopping in its lyricism, a rebirth.

'You're mine now,' he told her quietly. 'Mine. For
all your life.'

CHAPTER SEVEN

IN the distance flames leapt in a fiery holocaust, a devil's inferno against the purple-black sky. The smell was fantastic, evoking memories in Jane of burning the sugar when she was trying to make toffee. It was rich and syrupy and so sweet it was sickening. Yet she couldn't move away from the upstairs balcony even though her eyes smarted with smoke. The wind had changed direction and now that overwhelming caramel smell wafted in great waves towards the house.

They were filming the firing; a deliberate piece of spectacle and Jane could image its impact on the audience. Fire at any time was frightening, exciting, and over the burning fields the sky was red and studded with rainbow-coloured sparks. Sometimes those sparks escaped but men were on hand to see they died quickly. The filming would go on for hours and the fires had to be kept roaring.

Liz and Bryan had gone down to join Perry. Marina had retired early with a splitting headache and complaining of the burnt-toffee smell and Jane had elected to watch it all from the balcony. She knew perfectly well that had she gone closer her eyes would have been affected and the riding-scene was coming up in the morning. In it she was required to ride side-saddle and Alex had been helping her perfect her seat. There were many photographs of the McGovern women on horseback, one wearing a costume almost identical with the one Jane was to wear in the film, but none of a little English governess.

The Signora moved so soundlessly she might have

been a ghost. Jane failed to see or hear anything until the old lady came to stand beside her.

'Dante's Inferno!' she croaked in her foreign English voice.

'It's quite fantastic! It's almost turning night into an incredible rosy dawn.'

'You don't mind the smell?'

'It reminds me of when I was a little girl trying to make toffees for a school fete. Sugar burning in the bottom of a saucepan. Let me get you a chair, Signora.'

'Thank you.' The old lady inclined her imperious head. Tonight she was wearing another of her floor-length gowns, increasing Jane's sense of slipping back into the past.

As the Signora sat, Jane sat also, spacing the chintz-upholstered rattan chairs at a comfortable distance.

'Sandro has told me everything,' the old lady suddenly announced.

Everything? Not only the flames but the bright crimson colour scorched Jane's creamy skin.

'I've eaten nothing since he told me.'

'Are you so distressed, Signora, that we have fallen in love? Neither of us intended it.'

'If you think that will help me, my dear, it doesn't. There is much to admire about you. You are a beautiful and talented young lady. You are courteous, considerate and you handle yourself well. My son and his wife are very much on your side. You are the kind of young women who fits very easily into this environment. You ride, you swim, you appear to take a great interest in the plantation and the people who work for us. The staff would do anything for you when they would not for Antonella who is family.'

Jane could scarcely point out that Antonella didn't exactly endear herself to anybody with her egocentric and extremely autocratic manner. Born to a very wealthy family her old-style arrogance didn't go down well in a relatively classless society.

Even then the Signora voiced Jane's thoughts. 'Antonella comes from a very distinguished family,' she pointed out severely. 'It is difficult for ordinary people to understand her.'

'I understand her well enough, Signora,' Jane countered quietly.

'Your family? We know nothing of them.'

'Nor they of you.' Compared with the McGoverns, Jane could only see her family as utterly perfect.

'Your father, he does what?'

'My father is a senior partner in a firm of barristers and solicitors. Surely you've overheard my mentioning this to Helen?' She was quite certain the old lady had done so. 'My eldest brother, Nick, has followed Father into the same firm and my young brother, Grant, is what he always wanted to be, a veterinarian.'

'Really?' The old lady looked singularly unimpressed. 'Your mother would not condone what you are doing were she here.'

'My mother, Signora, is a woman of wisdom and understanding. She would be as supportive as she has always been in the past. She would be worried too.'

'On what score?' The old lady looked affronted.

'This is a very tempestuous household, especially when your young relative is visiting. She has been abominably rude to me since she first laid eyes on me and I was a complete stranger.'

'So?' The jet-black eyes flashed. 'Don't we women have uncanny intuition? Antonella divined you would cause unhappiness and great bitterness.'

'Because Alex has fallen in love with me?'

'Are you quite sure of that?' The old lady turned her snow-white head.

'As sure as you are, Signora, which is why you have sought me out.'

'There has been no one in Toni's life but Sandro,' the old lady muttered bleakly.

'But that's not true, is it?' Jane tried to balance respect with a healthy show of spirit. 'Antonella on her own admission has had many admirers.' She refrained from saying lovers.

'They are as nothing to my Sandro.' The Signora hunched her frail shoulders contemptuously. 'I have always acted in what I considered to be the best interests of my family. I idolise my grandson. I am very fond of Antonella. I ask you to believe when she is happy there is no who would be sweeter or more obedient. You have made her very unhappy.'

'Perhaps, Signora, you too might take a little of the blame?' Jane managed quietly.

'I don't understand what you're talking about,' the old lady returned harshly.

'I was hoping you would.' Jane looked down carefully at her clenched hands. 'Situations can be created. You just said you make plans. Antonella has been very much affected by the plans that you made. You've been arranging her marriage since she was a child. You've spoken to her of it. It was highly likely she would grow up thinking that in good time whe would marry Alex.'

'And she will, if you will permit it.'

'I don't believe that,' Jane said.

'That doesn't surprise me. You are young. You know very little. You think the only thing in life is how Alex feels about you, now. He would move heaven and earth to have you. But can you really see yourself fitting into this family?'

'Forgive me, Signora,' Jane said quietly, 'but you can't decide Alex's wife. He's not some malleable young man. He's a very forceful character in his own right. You've done everything in your considerable power to bring about a match. I understand Antonella makes a long visit each year and Alex keeps very much in touch with his Italian relations. Yet Alex has never spoken one word of love, or marriage.'

'You know this?' The old lady gave a funny little barking laugh.

'Alex told me what he feels for his cousin is a deep affection, not love,' Jane said staunchly.

'You think marriages are not successful based on deep affection?' the Signora countered. 'Mine was, and it was perfect. You don't hear of marriages breaking up when the partners are filled with deep affection. They are good friends. It is important to share the same background, the same interests, the same goals. It is important to be supported by family. Families hold marriages together. Family is more lasting than passion, lust, whatever. Anyone of any experience knows this.'

'And you in your wisdom have decided what is right for Alex?'

'How dare you speak to me like that!' Anger was stamped all over Signora's autocratic face.

'I regret upsetting you, Signora. I was brought up to respect my elders, but I'm not so spineless that I will allow myself to be crushed. I love Alex. I've experienced deep affection. There is no possible point of comparison. No deep affection, no long-time friendship prepared me for what I feel now. I'm a different person.'

'So you don't think——' the old lady threw her hands up to the sky '——these fireworks will last? They will burn themselves out.'

Jane withdrew a little but she didn't fold. 'And you're quite certain Antonella is the sort of woman

Alex wants and needs? You're happy with her character, her attitudes, her whole style. It doesn't perturb you a little that she displays no generosity of nature, that she scorns communication with anyone she considers beneath her, that from time to time she appears to be somewhat unstable?'

'You are an observer of the faults and foibles of others, are you?'

'I cannot be anything else when Antonella goes out of her way to be so—unsympathetic. All the people here involved in the filming, she takes no notice of them. They don't exist. Her mind seems to centre entirely on her own affairs. After Carol was brought back from hospital she expressed no concern. She seemed to isolate herself from what had happened when everyone else, including you, Signora, was terribly upset. Antonella affects a hypersophisticated manner, but it seems to me she has considerable maturing to do. Her aggression, her hostility towards me is intolerable from a civilised woman. If she is so much the aristocrat, why doesn't she act like one?'

'For the very reason sexual hostility is the most potent, the most dangerous in the world. We all know of crimes of passion,' the old lady said harshly. 'What is your film, if not the love of two women for one man? How do we know the role you are playing is far from the truth? No one knows what happened to the Contessa. It was thought she was attacked and killed by a crazed kanaka but her body was never found. In such a place, even now, one could very easily dispose of a body.'

'You're not suggesting the governess had anything to do with it?' Jane knew a moment of violent recoil.

'Very likely not,' the Signora said raspingly, 'but because of her, the Contessa, a woman of my own family, died. One has only to look into the eyes in her portrait to realise the unhappiness she was experiencing.'

'Could it not have been because she felt cut off from everything she knew? I know John McGovern built her a magnificent villa but when she looked out from her balcony it wasn't on civilised grandeur, the beauty and dignity of a great and wealthy European city. She looked out on primitive splendour—the jagged monolith, Monteverdi, the rain-forest, the jungle, the brilliant blue bay and the hundreds of tropical islands beyond. There would have been no other women of her class and station. She bore two children at a time and in a place where the mortality rate was appallingly high. She could have been ill, for all we know. She could have been suffering from a severe depression. She could, for that matter, have taken her own life.'

'Taken her own life?' The Signora turned on Jane, confounded. 'Never has such a thing been suggested.'

'Why not? She's trying to tell us something. If we look at this thing realistically, the mortality rate in the early days of the colony was appallingly high. Nearly every family lost a child, or children. It was a terrible fact of life. Especially in the tropics. One had to be very strong, or very lucky to survive, probably both. The Contessa in the portrait looks very frail as opposed to delicate or very slender. Can you imagine her fear if something went wrong with her? Something internal? Severe headaches? Something consistent that terribly disturbed her. It is even possible she may have thought of suicide as a way out.'

'Putting aside her husband, her children?' The Signora looked astounded.

'What if she thought her children would be looked after? What if she thought she couldn't bear to suffer or be a burden?'

'Why are you talking to me like this?' the Signora demanded looking painfully old and disturbed.

'Oh, please forgive me!' Jane was distressed.

'What you are making are groundless assumptions.'

'I realise that. It's only as I look up into the Contessa's eyes, I feel I am looking into the eyes of a woman who knows she is never to grow old.'

'Dear God! how you get carried away!'

'Don't you feel it?' Jane asked simply.

'Yes, I do.' The Signora was suddenly, abruptly, defeated and Jane sprang up.

'Please allow me to help you.'

'If you would be so kind.' The Signora grimaced. 'Of course there were deaths. Many deaths. But how could a woman keep such a thing from her husband? Surely she would confide in him her anxieties? Where would she go? What would she do? Do you realise a man died? So few people cared about a poor coloured man! He was never given an opportunity to tell his story when he became calm and rational. He was cut down by a small party of angry settlers. It is all too ... unthinkable, astounding, this theory.'

They were moving very slowly back into the house, the Signora, in her intense preoccupation, leaning heavily on Jane's arm.

'Were there no diaries, letters, Signora? Surely in those days a lonely, educated women would feel the need to commit her thoughts to paper. Wouldn't she write frequently to her family?'

'There were letters, certainly. Many, many letters. It was the other one, the governess who kept the diaries, the written accounts. She had no one to write to in England, only an aunt who died a short time after the girl sailed. She was good family, a young woman who never expected to become a servant, but the conditions of life can change very abruptly.'

'But I've never heard of these journals,' Jane was moved to exclaim in a shocked voice.

'And why would you hear?' the old lady countered harshly. 'Such things are not for your eyes. Who are you to be allowed to read such private papers?'

'Have you read them, Signora?' Jane demanded urgently.

'Why would I read them?' the old lady cried in disgust. 'She brought nothing but tragedy and grief to this family. Had I my way, those journals would have been destroyed.'

It was impossible to speak to Alex about the matter although it kept Jane tossing and turning for most of the night. The more she thought about it, the more she was convinced the Contessa had not only been unhappy, but ill. Those great dark eyes haunted her and in the dead of night Jane wondered if some flickering shade of that tragic young women was trying to tell her descendants what they had always desperately wanted to know. A man had paid with his life for the Contessa's momentous disappearance and it was even possible if one believed in an after-life that the spirit of the Contessa would have knowledge of such things. Wrongs had to be set right.

'Why me?' Jane breathed into the darkness. 'Why me?' It was strange she was experiencing so much awareness when she wasn't family at all. She recalled her grandmother on her mother's side had an uncanny sensitivity that briefly startled them from time to time. She seemed to know a few seconds before the phone rang which member of the family or close friend would call; when any one of them was in trouble. She had predicted a devoted friend's fatal car-accident and had recognised the phone call from the hospital for what it was. Her father called Nanna Elsa a witch and, affectionately as he said it, with a glint of amusement, the whole family acknowledged there was

more than a hint of truth in it. Some people were
gifted—or cursed—with exceptional psychic powers.
Jane thought something of that must be happening to
her now. She dozed fitfully for the rest of the night
and even when she slept her dreams were invaded by
shadowy figures and questions. Had anyone bothered
to read the English governess's journals? Or had she
been put on trial and condemned once and for all?

Alex, when he saw her pale face and shadowed eyes,
thought it would be best if they put off the riding-
scene.

'Actually those shadowed eyes are terrific!' Perry
was only concerned for the film. 'She's unhappy, isn't
she? Fearful of what is happening to her. You're okay,
aren't you, Jane?'

'I'm fine.' Jane was anxious to have the scene shot.
Her bad night would have to account for her fluttery
nerves.

'You don't look fine to me.' Alex looked down at her
sharply, a frown between his winged, black brows.
'Didn't you sleep well?'

'Not really.'

'Was it the firing, the smoke and the smell?'

'A few things on my mind.' Jane gave him a slight
smile. 'Don't worry, Alex. I can handle it.'

'And I'm right here to see that you can,' he said
forcefully. 'I don't know what to make of Wyndham.
He can't take his eyes off you yet he's prepared to let
you do a difficult stunt under par.'

'I can handle it, Alex,' Jane repeated, the tilt of her
head indicating a girl from make-up was approaching.
'I'm a good rider and you've coached me very well.'

'I don't like it,' Alex persisted almost wrathfully.
'Why not a stand-in?'

'We've been over this before.' This morning her

clear green eyes had turned a dark jade. 'We've rehearsed it and it went perfectly each time. Anyway I feel quite confident with you on hand.'

'I saddled the mare up myself. Only you're such a good horsewoman I wouldn't let you do it.' Alex stepped back as the make-up girl closed in to check Jane's hair and face.

'Perfect, Miss Gilmour. Good luck now,' she smiled.

'Thanks, Glenny.' Jane tilted her head and drew a deep, steadying breath. 'I'd better go, Alex. Perry is about ready to roll.'

'He'll get clobbered if you so much as bruise an elbow,' Alex returned briefly. A certain tension was on him that found an answering chord in Jane and he bent his head in front of all of them and kissed her cheek. 'I'm here. Behind the scenes. I'll have my eye on your every second and I have Sultan saddled up.'

'What more could I want?' Jane looked through her heavy lashes into his high-mettled, handsome face. 'There's something I want to talk to you about afterwards.'

'I'll be here.' He spread his hands in a truly Latin gesture. 'Take care, Gianina. Can I be blamed if I'm anxious? You're everything in the world to me.'

'Alex?' Her hand came out and fastened on his wrist. 'Do you mean that?'

'You don't believe it?' There was a kind of impatience in his brilliant blue eyes.

'I say, you two,' Liz was rushing towards them, the morning breeze in her dark helmet of hair, 'Perry is ready for Jane now.'

'Coming.'

'You look, good, Janey,' Liz announced. 'Very good. That pale face is a nice touch.'

'It's not a touch, it is pale,' Alex clipped off.

'Listen, dear,' Liz turned to him in a motherly fashion, 'why don't you go off while this scene is being shot? We'll all see not the slightest harm comes to Jane.'

'Maybe you will, but I'm staying,' Alex confirmed. 'Jane won't be going anywhere near that cliff but I'm not taking even the slightest chance. You people allow too much drama to spill over into real life. I even believe Wyndham would deliberately put Jane into some danger to add authenticity to the scene.'

'Oh, Alex!' Liz's mouth opened to protest, but just at that moment Perry bellowed,

'Could I have Miss Gilmour here?'

'Let's get it over!' Jane breathed. 'I'm terribly hot in this long fitted habit.'

'Actually you look marvellously cool,' Liz said as they moved off. 'I can understand Alex not wanting you to take risks, but you're so good and we have everything set up. It's marvellous what can be faked. You fail to take the fence and there are a pile of mattresses on the other side.'

From the beginning Alex had opposed the idea of Jane's faking a fall—there were stunt women to do it—but none oddly enough more convincing than Jane.

'A real professional!' Perry dubbed her even if Alex once told him bluntly Jane could very well break her neck for the sake of the picture.

Alex had chosen a chestnut mare from his own stable, a beautiful-looking animal, for the filming and docile enough to present little threat to Jane, side-saddle.

From the moment she was up, Jane sensed a subtle difference.

'Ready when you are, Jane.'

She opened her mouth to voice her faint unease, then shut it again. The three camera-men were in position and Josh was ready with his clapper-board. She let the mare catch sight of the whip—it was necessary to establish control and the mare seemed to settle.

'Take 1, Scene 540!'

Jane moved off. The particular scene called for an early morning encounter between Ogilvie and his children's governess; an encounter that had its moment of drama as Laura's mare threw her at the ruins of a stone wall. It had been rehearsed with a stunt woman many times and Jane looking on had come to the conclusion she could do it herself. In fact she took a perfectly convincing dive without hurting herself at all.

This morning she was nervous and perhaps as a consequence the mare's placidity had left her.

Perry positively shouted to 'Cut!'

Take 2.

The mare exhaled noisily.

Take 3.

Jane leaned down and just flicked the mare's side.

It was the start of some of the most terrifying moments of Jane's life.

The mare responded to the signal, knowing full well what was required, but as Jane urged it to the gallop it unleashed a frenzy of speed, heading not in the direction of the cameras but towards the thick, bordering area of eucalypts and paperbarks.

It was trying to throw her off!

Burdened as she was by a long habit and even more by the long-discarded method of riding Jane felt almost unequal to the task of controlling the frenzied animal.

She was sweating and so was the horse. They were racing towards the trees where any one of the low-growing branches could whip her off.

She pulled hard on the reins, hurting the mare's sensitive mouth, and like a miracle it slowed then began to go into a series of bucking movements.

'Hang on, Jane!' A man's voice yelled.

Jane tried desperately to retain her seat while the mare bucked tirelessly, a wild brumby and not a beautiful, sweet-tempered blood-horse. It was obvious something was driving it mad.

Jane was so engrossed in trying to bring the thrashing animal under control she was scarcely aware of the swiftly approaching horse and rider. Her own beautiful mount was a killer, an explosion of powerful legs and gleaming hoofs and in another moment it would dislodge her. It was a tribute to her skill that she had managed to stay on so long.

'*Here, Gianina!*'

As suddenly as it had begun it was all but over. Alex hauled her from her horse, getting such a crushing grip on her she thought she cracked a rib.

'God almighty!' His breath whistled in her ear.

She couldn't answer, her head fallen sideways while her body tried frantically to adjust itself to Sultan's momentum.

They were coming; all of them, converging on the spot.

'My God, what a performance!' Perry cried.

It was quite the wrong thing to say. Alex, who was kneeling on the ground beside Jane, holding her head down as a wave of nausea passed over her, looked up abruptly, murder in blue eyes that were set in a face of carved stone.

'My darling girl!' Liz flung herself down on the other side. 'Whatever went wrong?'

'Now *I'd* say the bloody horse went mad!' Bryan shuddered. He was genuinely very fond of Jane and he just couldn't believe what he had just seen. It was almost as if someone had replaced the mare with a rogue horse. And a killer at that!

'I'm all right.'

'The hell you are! You look ghastly.' Alex fingered her costume, loosening folds and buttons.

'Ah, that's better!' Jane let out a long sigh.

Someone from the plantation had caught the mare and now he came to Alex, going down on his knees beside him, speaking very rapidly in a low voice, in Italian.

None of them understood a word, but they understood the expression on Alex McGovern's face. He was thunderstruck. Then violently he twisted up.

'What was all that about?' Liz breathed.

'Something they didn't want us to know,' Bryan answered, very drily. 'How are you now, love?'

'I think I've broken a rib.' Jane winced. Nearly every pin in her head had been shaken out and now her ash-gold hair fell in great loops.

'I feel so responsible!' Liz choked.

'I'll be damned if McGovern isn't the most dynamic man I've ever met!' Perry exclaimed in unwilling admiration. 'He just vaulted into the saddle and took off while the rest of us were just wondering if something had gone wrong. The hell of it is, we can't use it. A scene like that lives in the mind.'

'Jane could have been killed!' Bryan muttered darkly. Liz, too, had stiffened, looking around at Perry with considerable distaste.

'Of course I was terrified for Jane.' When Perry spoke again it was with the utmost concern. 'Unless I'm very much mistaken McGovern is conducting some kind of investigation. There should never have been a problem. He hand-picked the animal himself and up to date it's behaved beautifully.'

'You'll have to have an X-ray, Jane,' Liz was saying quietly. 'Might as well call it off, Perry, for the rest of the day.'

CHAPTER EIGHT

ALEX drove her to the hospital and waited while she was given a thorough examination. No ribs had been broken and all she had to show for her few minutes of heart-stopping fright was an area of deep discoloration beneath her right breast.

'Whatever happened?' the doctor asked her. 'I think it very strange your horse would react like that unless it was in pain. Has Alex checked it?'

'I'm sure he has.' Jane buttoned up her blouse and stepped from behind the screen. He was so upset and angry I dared not ask him.'

'A very complex man is Alex.' The doctor looked up at her curiously. 'I've known him from the day he was born. I delivered him as a matter of fact. In some ways he's the image of his father—a magnificent man—yet he's much more complicated. The whole town knows he's very impressed with you.'.

'And do they approve?' Jane asked with grave seriousness.

'My dear, why wouldn't they?' Dr McNeill countered gallantly. 'You're a very beautiful young lady and, from what I hear, very talented.'

'The work is getting harder,' Jane smiled, a lovely illumination in her pale, strained face. 'Thank you very much, Doctor. With a clean bill-of-health filming will resume tomorrow.'

'Can't you give it another day?' Dr McNeill suggested.

'Our director hates delays,' Jane explained. 'We're almost through location work. The rest of the filming—scenes with the children, interior—will be shot in Sydney.'

'I hope they pay you well.'

'They do, and we're under budget, at least for now. Being allowed to film on the estate was the biggest thing that has happened to us.

'No one jealous of you, is there?'

The doctor didn't sound as if he were joking and Jane spun around.

'Jealous?'

'Jealous of the leading ladies.' Dr McNeill gave a gruff laugh. 'I enjoy Angela Lansbury in that *Murder She Wrote*. Someone is always getting rid of someone.'

'You are joking, aren't you, Doctor?' Jane stared up into his face.

''Course I am, m'dear. I couldn't stand it, if I weren't. I haven't forgotten that whole sorry business with your little friend—what was her name, the actress?'

'Carol Graham.'

'Very pretty girl. I've treated plenty of spider-bites over the years, but I've never heard of one sitting in the parlour so to speak.'

'Did you say this to Alex?'

'Matter of fact, I did. Same as I'm going to say to him now. Horses are unpredictable animals but I'd go looking for the cause. Obviously it was trying to throw you because it couldn't bear to carry you.'

'So?'

'So, it could very well have been in pain.'

They had a late lunch in the town; a picturesque little restaurant overlooking the shimmering blue bay.

'How are you feeling now?' There was a faint pallor beneath Alex's darkly golden tan, a harshness to his expression.

'Not bad. Not bad at all.'

'You don't complain, do you?'

'I'm just so grateful you were on hand.'

'To nearly crack your ribs?' He looked away abruptly over the sparkling water.

'It was a panic situation, remember? You had to get me off the mare any way you could.'

'I don't think I'll forget it for many a long year.' He sat looking sombrely at a distant island. 'It was deliberate, you know.'

'I thought it might be,' Jane said quietly. 'I noticed something wrong from the moment I was in the saddle. I should have checked.'

He turned his sculptured head to look at her. 'There's a shrub up here called the Stinging Tree. The leaves and stems are covered with stiff hairs and each hair has a sharp point that contains a poison. The stings are extremely painful and the effects can last for weeks. Someone put a large leaf between the folds of the horse blanket. The mare could only tolerate the pain up to a certain point then she went berserk.'

'Dear God!' Jane exclaimed softly, then remained quiet. She knew that 'someone' had to be Antonella but it would be very painful for Alex to accept it.

But he turned his face to her, not shrinking from it. 'Of course it had to be Antonella,' he said tonelessly.

'It would be difficult to think of anyone else.'

'I could kill her!' he said with sudden explosiveness.

'Alex!' Jane was surprised and a little frightened by the savagery in his voice.

'So now you're going to defend her?'

'I'd have to be very sure it *was* Antonella.'

'You could have been killed, Jane,' he pointed out very quietly, a primitive anger behind the patrician façade.

'It was a terrible thing for her to do. If she did it.'

'Who else would have the slightest reason to harm

you? We must assume now that she has tried before. That business with Carol—it was meant for you. I told myself for all her faults she couldn't possibly do such a thing. Yet the fear remained. I thought I'd done everything in my power to keep you safe. No one was allowed near the stables. No one. Since the filming I've had extra staff patrolling the estate, a lot of extra staff, yet somehow she slipped through.'

'It looks like we're condemning her on intuition alone.' Jane was moved to pity.

'If she's guilty, I'll get it out of her,' he vowed with deadly quietness. 'No one will stop me. Antonella has never moved beyond the security of family. In a sense we have pandered to her at the expense of her moral development. Every one of us is guilty of not allowing her to mature as she should. Instead of holding her accountable for certain aspects of her behaviour, we've persuaded ourselves they were only phases to be worked through. She has been over-indulged to such an extent that all that exists for her is self-gratification. She has never even begun to learn tolerance. She thinks she can sweep through life with no thought for anyone but herself. You say she loves me—is in love with me—it is more a blind refusal to accept there is one man she can't have. For one so young Antonella is an inveterate seductress and she has been heavily influenced by the circle she moves in. When she saw I was attracted to you she was moved to aggression. Now it controls her. She will have to go home and she will have to be punished.' His blue eyes blazed significantly.

'I don't think I want to be here when that happens.'

'It will not affect you.'

'Maybe not, if I can keep out of the way, but it will affect your grandmother. She wants you to marry Antonella.'

'And she has been getting what she wants for a long time,' Alex pointed out quite unexpectedly, his expression so taut his skin seemed stretched tight over his finely chiselled bones. 'When this filming is over I would like you to meet my mother. I dream of taking you to see her. She is a beautiful, gentle woman. Her goodness shines out of her. Yet she couldn't live here with Nonna. When my father was killed it was like a nightmare. None of us could believe it—accept it— and afterwards the bond between Nonna and my mother was broken. Nonna became as you see her now, very autocratic and severe, and my mother became so desperately unhappy she was forced to go. It was difficult for me too. I wanted to go with her, but there was Monteverdi.'

'I understand, Alex.' Jane's green eyes were soft and troubled.

'I know.' He gave her a tight, unhappy, yet dazzling smile. 'I've told Nonna she was quite wrong to put ideas into Antonella's head. I told her I loved you and I'm going to have you. I have waited a long time.'

'And how did she take that?'

'The customary severity. She is old. She is tired. She lost her beloved son, now her hopes for her grandson have come to nothing.'

'So it makes it very, very awkward, not to say impossible.'

'I won't pretend it's not a little awkward——' he gave a Gallic shrug '—but I mean what I say. The thing is, Gianina, what do *you* mean?'

'You know I love you.'

'Look at me then.'

'I might cry.'

'And I would pick you up and make love to you.'

She had to smile. 'At least not until we leave the restaurant.'

'You're finished, aren't you?'

'My coffee's gone cold.'

'If I could just have you to myself!' The flame was back in his eyes again.

'I'd like that.' She gave a funny little laugh that was almost a sob.

'Gianina,' he stood up and held out his hand, 'come now.'

The sun was blazing outside and they walked across the courtyard to the parking-area beyond.

In the car he leant across and kissed her mouth with driving hunger. 'I think you must come to me tonight.'

'No!'

'But why not?'

'I want to more than you'll ever know.'

'But you won't come to me until I marry you. Is that it?' He held her chin and kissed her again.

'Would you marry me, Alex?' She stared into his blue eyes.

'When, don't you mean?'

'When would be the right time?'

His smile had vanished utterly. 'This film could start you on a career. You have a certain something beyond beauty and talent. The camera follows you lovingly. It even catches the soul in your eyes. You see yourself in the rushes. Wyndham watches you like a star in the making. His star. Isn't he always saying you're right for the "big-time". What is this "big-time"? Do you really want to be a film star?'

'I've never wanted to be one,' Jane pointed out. 'Playing Laura was inescapable. The truth of the matter is I feel I'm being directed. Your grandmother told me there were journals, diaries, that have never been read.'

'I know nothing about them!'

There was no denying the sincerity of his expression. 'But your grandmother said they existed.'

'You mean, of the Contessa?'

'I mean of the young Englishwoman who wrote them, long ago. A young woman who had to give up her home, her country, her heart, even her reputation. She must have suffered a lot for the Contessa's tragedy. And she wasn't the only one who paid for it. I suggested to your grandmother the Contessa in her portrait not only looks unhappy, she looks as if she knows her life is almost over.'

'And it was,' he pointed out harshly.

'Perhaps not in the way you think. The thought drives me that she might have been ill. Incurably ill.'

'Easy, little one.' He soothed her with his hand.

'Can't we find the journals, Alex? Can't we read them? They might tell us something we need to know.'

'It's possible my grandmother simply made that up. God knows if such journals exist she has kept them a secret long enough.'

'I think she was telling the truth, Alex.'

'I can't believe it!' He looked both amazed and angry.

'So ask her.'

He gave a her a cool, hard smile. 'I will.'

Shooting went on through the afternoon, the difficult and terrible scene when the crazed kanaka was hunted down and suffered a rough justice. Umpteen takes were required and Perry was on the verge of losing all patience.

'It's tremendously important to get this right!' he yelled and even Liz turned away with a shudder.

'Kind of gruesome, isn't it?'

'I think I'll go back up to the house,' Jane agreed.

'Do that, sweetie, you're very pale. Another couple

of days will wrap it up here. Alex found out anything about the mare?'

'There was a burr caught on its blanket,' Jane explained with false calm. 'No one noticed and of course it dug in.'

'A burr?' Liz's dark eyebrows rose to her fringe. 'How the devil did it get there?'

'There are burrs everywhere, I suppose.' Jane tried to sound as off-hand as she could. 'I should have checked myself. I realised something was wrong immediately I was mounted but I didn't want to delay the shooting.'

'Well,' Liz looked highly sceptical, 'I must say plenty of them have caught on my jeans. But it was very careless of the attendant to say the least. I should think Alex will skin him alive. He's gone to such lengths to look after you—look after us all!'

'You know what they say,' Jane shrugged philosophically. 'All's well that ends well. I'll go and relax while I can.'

'You bet!' Liz patted her on the shoulder and hurried off.

At dinner Perry went into rhapsodies of praise about the filming so far.

'Of course I know I've been very hard on you from time to time, but the striving for perfection is showing.'

'How fascinating!' Antonella said.

'That's a sensational dress you're wearing, dear,' Marina purred. 'I just love the way it shows all your . . . assets.'

'You are so sweet. I have been thinking all this time you are marvellous for your age.'

'Twenty-nine, to be exact.'

'And you promised you wouldn't tell!' Bryan,

sandwiched between them, tried for the light touch. 'Thank God I'm working well. The novel is coming along in leaps and bounds. Something about the atmosphere, I think. It's very conducive to drama.'

'When am I going to read it?' Liz demanded.

'Not until I'm past the half-way mark.'

'Great!' There was pleasure and pride in Liz's face. 'I've always believed you had a lot more in you. As for the script! It might have left you exhausted but no one could have done it better.'

'I'll drink to that!' Perry raised his wine-glass.

As soon as dinner was over, Alex carried Jane off.

'I've spoken to Nonna,' he told her. 'She's enormously agitated about this, but I must look at it in a different way. It astounds me these journals have been left unread for more than a hundred years. It has taken you, a young woman from the other side of the world, a stranger up until a few short months ago, even to suggest their existence.'

'But then, the English governess was pushed into a closet. No one wanted to know about her. Although John McGovern loved her and indeed married her, she was the least acceptable member of this family. Your grandmother is of the Contessa's family and culture. It's understandable, I suppose, her attitude would be animosity-laden. She has known of the existence of those journals which may well tell us nothing about the disappearance of the Contessa, but she has never permitted herself to read them.'

'Nor anyone else,' Alex said sombrely. 'I'm sure my father never knew of their existence yet we've lived with the old scandal for so long. The descendants of the islander who was killed still live in the district. So many people, generations affected. This is a small world and conflicts last a long time. It is my opinion the whole tragedy was dealt with in the worst possible way, but then I suppose I am looking at it from the viewpoint of contemporary society. Even in the wilds the early settlers adhered to rigid codes of morality. My great-great grandfather suffered and so did both his wives.'

The tower-room where Alex led her was off in the west wing and reached by a narrow, curving flight of stone steps.

'Watch the hem of your dress, Jane.'

'Isn't there another light here, Alex?'

'I'm looking for it. I haven't been up here in years.'

'I can't see a thing.'

'Keep hold of my hand.' He drew her up to another landing and in the next moment a light flared. 'Perhaps you should have taken that dress off. It'll be dusty.'

'It will wash.' Jane looked down briefly at her imperial-yellow silk. She could barely contain her excitement and impatience. Who knew what they could find?

The door loomed in a stone archway, heavy, brass-bound, and Alex went forward and inserted a huge, antique key in the lock.

Jane fully expected the heavy old door to creak and groan, instead it seemed to float open and the muted golden light from the landing incongruously made the shadows dance.

Her heart began to pound.

'What is it, darling?'

'Nothing.' She shivered. Her skin was prickling.

'If you'd rather *I* looked.' His brilliant blue eyes marked the changing expressions on her face.

'No, I want to come with you.'

'There's nothing to harm you here, Gianina. I will never let anything harm you. In this world, or the next.'

'Hold me close for a moment,' she begged him a little breathlessly.

'I will hold you, forever!' His voice was neither tender nor solicitous but ringing with possession.

'Alex?' She turned up her mouth and she saw his passion for her blaze out of his eyes.

His hand grasped her silky hair and he locked her to him. 'You're my prisoner.'

'That's the way it was meant to be.'

'I want you more than I ever thought it possible. You are perfect to me.'

'But there doesn't seem much we can do about it right now.' A faint melancholy look caught in her luminous green eyes.

He gave a hard, brief laugh. 'My darling girl, anyone who cares to cross me—watch out. When this filming is over you are going to marry me. It will be a big wedding. Everything you want. Whatever you desire, I swear I will get. I can deny you nothing. Your parents, your family, they must have a little time. Of course we will fly them here. My mother will come to us. She will love you for you have her gentleness of nature.'

'And Antonella? Your grandmother? They are still here.' Silently Jane laid her face against his heart.

'Tell me that's the way it's going to be, Gianina.' He tugged very gently on her hair, forcing her to look at him.

'I love you.' Her voice was so soft, so faintly hollow it sounded like an echo.

'Does loving me make you sad?'

'I love you so much.' With her head tilted back her blonde hair flowed over her shoulders.

'Your expression is exquisite.' His dark, handsome face became very grave and intent. 'I was thinking what my ancestor must have thought when he saw his English governess for the first time. If he felt the way I felt about you he could never have hoped to live happily ever after. Passion, true passion, is simply too different from devotion. I don't think I want to read these journals, Gianina. Perhaps you feel the same way.'

'I know she was innocent,' Jane murmured and her lovely eyes filled with tears. 'They were all innocent, Alex. Can you doubt it?'

'Innocence is expected of a woman. A man can be violent. Have you thought how I would react if someone tried to take you from me?'

'Yes, I've thought about it,' she said. 'You are a very formidable man. You might take instant action— you are brave. But you would never do anything weak or cowardly. Of that, I'm very sure. You would look at the situation and overcome it.'

'So!' He bent his head and kissed her mouth. 'I've long given up trying to fathom what really happened. These journals might only increase the mystery, or they could be a disaster.'

'I'm not afraid.'

'Well then.' He lifted his raven-dark head, his smile a little twisted. 'I suppose we'll have to read them.'

They weren't easy to find. In fact Alex's grand-mother had deliberately set them a daunting task. The impressively sized room was crammed with furniture; ornate gilded mirrors, stacks of paintings with elaborate frames; valuable antiques jostling back to back. There was such a profusion, at first glance Jane thought it might take a day just to clear a path but it seemed a strong man could move very heavy objects at will. While she stood wondering where best to start, Alex set about overcoming the problems; removing dust-sheets, shifting desks, chests, chairs, a Louis Quinze-style bureau which looked like Kingwood with the finest quality ormolu.

'This is fantastic!' Jane breathed. 'There's enough here to open an antique shop.'

'Most of it is the real thing,' he said carelessly. 'That bureau is Boulle.'

'Then what's it doing here?'

'Someone didn't like it, I suppose.' He stopped and let his eyes range over the room. 'When I was a boy, my mother showed me a portrait of your governess. My mother couldn't see any bad in anyone. I guess it must still be here.'

'My God, Alex!' Jane, who had been staring absently at all the unwanted treasures, started up.

'Little one, your face had gone stark white.'

'Where would it be?' she cried.

'Here, sit down. The sofa looks all right.' He moved back and took her shoulder, pressing her down on to a Rococo-style settee, elaborately fretted and carved.

'No, I'll help you find it.'

'You'll sit there,' he told her with considerable firmness. 'All this filming makes me a little angry. You might be an excellent actress but it doesn't seem to agree with you. You're up too early. You go to bed too late. In between Wyndham works you too hard. He is rather an insensitive man.'

'Was she beautiful?' Jane asked.

'A *femme fatale*. I remember thinking that. Nonna said, how dared my mother show it to me? My father shrugged it aside. I think he too was attracted by her.' As he spoke he was working steadily towards a stack of large paintings.

'This is a week of surprises,' Jane said. 'First, the journals. Now, a portrait. Why was it never mentioned before? Liz would love to see it.'

'Liz is not going to see it,' he said. 'Such things are for family.' He extended his arm and began to move the heavy paintings forward, while Jane edged towards him, considerably shaken.

He stopped. There was a brief silence, then he spoke. 'Here it is.'

'Please, Alex, I long to see it.'

'Why would you not? The first time I saw you I thought; it is only a dream.'

'Alex?'

He moved the canvas sideways so that the subject came into view. A white silky gown, dusky pink drapery, a wrist, an almost cuff-like gold bracelet set with a huge garnet cabochon and flanked by smaller stones inlaid with diamonds, a lovely, long-fingered white hand.

'Do you see her now?'

'Not quite.'

He pushed the painting further and now Jane saw a pale, composed face looking straight at her. The expression was soft, sweet, warm. The eyes were large, grey, glowing, the skin mother-of-pearl. The abundant hair was an ash-gold, the elegant, delicate bones held an underlying strength. There was a faint smile on the softly moulded lips.

I know her, Jane thought.

'It must be strange to see your double,' Alex said almost crisply. 'They say we have one in this world.'

'Alex!'

'You don't recognise yourself?'

'How strange we're so much alike!'

His brilliant eyes gleamed. 'All the years she's spent up here! When I was a boy, for long after I first saw her, I used to imagine I could hear her crying. I was an imaginative child.'

'Look into her eyes.'

'I have.'

'Then you believe in her?'

'I suppose, underneath, I've always been trying to defend her.'

'Do you think the journals would be locked away in that bureau?' Jane indicated the French cylinder-top desk.

'I don't think so.' Alex gave it only a cursory glance. 'I seem to remember it downstairs in my grandfather's day.'

'Didn't your grandmother tell you exactly where?'

'She's very much against our finding them at all. Nonna favours making things difficult. I didn't press her beyond making her admit they were here. In this room. Now that I've seen it again I plan to have it cleared out. A lot of this is much sought-after. I have a special scheme going for the children of the district. We'll arrange an auction and put the proceeds to a clubhouse.'

In the end it was Jane who opened a nineteenth-century dome-top travelling-trunk covered in tooled leather. She knew before she touched them she had found the journals.

'Alex!'

He swung about, alerted by the soft urgency of her tone. 'Found them, have you?'

'I think so.' Though she spoke so quietly her eyes were huge.

'Then we'll take them downstairs.' He straightened up, then abruptly lifted his head. 'Did you hear anything?' His handsome face was dangerously alert.

She stared at him. 'Your nerves are a bit jumpy.'

'Not me!' He all but sprang past her and as he did, the massive wooden door slammed shut.

'Toni!' Now he was shouting. He turned the heavy knob but the door did not yield. 'You silly little fool!'

'God, Alex, has she locked us in?'

He gave a short laugh. 'I'd have a hard job knocking it down. I'll have to go out on the roof.'

'You're crazy! That would be dangerous.'

'You just leave that to me. I'm probably the fittest man you know.'

She was arrested by the truth of that. 'Well, be that as it may, you could spare a thought for me. I can't let you do it. It's pitch-black out there. You could miss your footing. You could fall!'

'I won't fall,' he told her briskly, cupping her face in his hands and giving her a typical dare-devil smile. 'There's a room directly beneath us with a balcony. James Bond wouldn't do it any better. If Toni thinks we might perish up here, she's got another think coming. I don't intend to sit around until someone thinks to look for us either. I'm going to get hold of that girl and give her a dozen hard whacks where it will do the most good. I've denied myself the pleasure for too long.'

'I think you must be raving mad. You could end up in hospital and a man like you would find it a crashing bore.'

'Darling, trust me.' His blue eyes glittered.

'What about if I put my head out the window and screamed?'

He gave a short, nasty laugh. 'Don't do that. I'm planning a little surprise.' He went to the window, opened it out, put one long leg over the sill and looked down. 'Piece of cake!'

'Alex, take care.' Her tone was one of flawless love and concern.

'I will, my love.' For an instant he allowed her hand to curl in his. 'Climbing down buildings is only one of my dazzling talents. Now, why don't you go back there and get those journals together. It will give you something to do so you won't go staring after me, and you and I are going to read them all—very carefully—tonight.'

CHAPTER NINE

Long weeks later in Sydney, Jane was still reliving those moments of petrifying fright when Alex scaled the roof of Monteverdi and dropped as lightly as a cat-burglar to the balcony beneath.

She had remained fixed at the window staring after him wondering how she had ever allowed him to do such a dangerous thing. She loved him more than she ever thought possible, more than life. Every other consideration, the finding of the diaries, her amazement at the portrait, her horror of the 'accidents' Antonella had arranged were submerged by her fear. When he had swung outwards before the drop, her heart had leapt to her throat. But he had only leaned back to wave almost carelessly before disappearing into the house.

That was then. Four hours later, all the outbursts had ceased. Antonella, wailing and protesting her innocence, had for once encountered a steel trap. The Signora finally had turned on her and given the order for her bags to be packed. Placing 'outsiders' in danger was one thing, placing her beloved grandson in jeopardy was unforgivable, for ever. Antonella had been banished, laughing hysterically, the tears streaming down her cheeks.

'Nonna, Nonna,' she had cried over and over but the old lady had only stared at her implacably as if she had never truly seen Antonella before in her life.

With every nerve quivering on the surface, Jane had turned to reading the journals with Alex. The Signora had remained in the room, hunched like some ancestor figure, hands clasped together, eyes burning black in a crumpled parchment face. Only then did she seem fearful of what she might hear now she knew that Antonella had indeed tried to harm Jane. Not once, but twice as Jane had long suspected.

Every word of those journals was cut into Jane's brain. Every lucid line erasing the obsessive hatred and bitterness that had accumulated with successive generations. Many passages Jane had read aloud while Alex watched her transparent face and the Signora, inscrutable, gazed blindly across the room.

Understanding had come late, very late. The English governess spoke often of watching her mistress standing on the upper balcony staring as if hypnotised out at the bay. Once the diary recorded she had speculated on whether 'death in the sea would be preferable to death on land'.

One of the diaries actually spoke of the Contessa's 'fainting-spells' when without warning she would pitch to the floor. It spoke of 'inexplicable mood changes': of the 'sweetest and gentlest of mothers' becoming strangely 'hostile' and unable to bear the 'high pitch' of the children's chatter. It spoke of increasing 'withdrawals' and a dependence on laudanum. It spoke of the household's efforts to restore the Contessa's interest in life and well-being. It speculated strongly on the relationship between a woman and her environment. It was obvious the English governess had taken the view her mistress had lost all sense of happiness and security in such an alien place. The striking feature was, no one seemed to have realised they were observing the behaviour of a woman who most probably was suffering the alienation of a terminal disease. Such recognition of classic symptoms is commonplace in the modern world but evidently it had not been comprehended at the time.

By the time they had finished reading there was unquestioning acceptance that the Contessa at the time of her tragic disappearance had been exhibiting the symptoms of a brain tumour or a cancer that was attacking the brain. Even the Signora had nodded her weary assent. There was far more reason to suppose the Contessa in her despair or under the influence of laudanum had simply walked out to sea rather than having become the victim of a crazed field-hand's attack.

That fateful night the Signora seemed consumed by a remorse so strong there was no way she wished to hang on to life. The shock of Antonella's aberrations— if indeed it *was* a shock—was nothing to the knowledge that she had allowed her family to go on suffering for a long, long time. She had been aware of the existence of the journals almost all her married life. She had stood in the way of two gentle ghosts, her own Contessa and the one she had always referred to scathingly as 'the English adventuress'. It had taken another young Englishwoman, a young woman she was opposed to, to get to the truth of the matter.

It was a highly emotional night and it emptied the reservoir of the Signora's strength. She was particularly quiet, almost conscience-stricken for a few days, then when one looked at it from the vantage point of hindsight she appeared to compose herself for the inevitable.

Alex found her seated in her favourite chair on the upper balcony looking sightlessly out over the bay. In a miraculous way, death had wiped out all the old bitterness and grief and her peaceful face held the imprint of her once striking beauty.

'I never thought I would be so upset!' Liz had wept. 'After all, she wasn't like any grannie I ever knew, but she really did live for her family.'

The family was devastated and Jane became haunted by the knowledge that her coming to Monteverdi had drastically altered too many lives. Antonella had been banished. The Signora had grown weary of life. Although Helen did her best to comfort her, no one could convince Jane she had not been the catalyst in the whole drama. Alex didn't even try.

Overnight he became subdued and remote. The surging need had turned to withdrawal.

It took another two months' shooting at their Sydney studios for the filming to be completed. Location work had brought tremendous realism to the film as well as keeping costs down but many scenes from the beginning and middle of the film, including all the scenes with the children, were shot in the studio buildings or in a Sydney mansion. Robert O'Donoghue, the editor, and Perry, as director, had already assembled a rough cut, but it would be many weeks, probably months before the final film was ready for the sneak preview. One of the country's top composers had already been hired, but as often happened had elected to wait until they returned to Sydney to begin work. Once he had absorbed period, mood, style, the score was actually completed in two months. The theme music, in particular, was ravishingly beautiful and haunting and Liz gleefully predicted a big hit. A big 'romantic' film called for significantly 'lush' music and they were all in agreement it was a magnificent score. All that remained was the complicated process of dubbing all the various separate sound-tracks into the master tape, which was then used to produce the composite sound-track.

Prisoner of the Sun was not expected to be released to the public until the film had been tested in a preview. Audience reaction often influenced the final editing. Also publicity and advertising, already begun, had to be given sufficient time to stimulate public interest. It was planned to issue a tape of the score and Frederic Armstrong's book, long out of print, was reissued in paperback with a shot of the three central characters, inevitably the 'love triangle' on the cover. Everything that would make people want to see the film had to be done and of course there was a huge party.

'Wear something sensational!' Liz advised Jane. 'Something to knock their eyes out. I know Marina plans to.'

'I don't know if I can face it,' Jane said simply.

'Darling, you've got to!' Liz cried dramatically. 'You're our star.'

'One of them.'

'An important one. Some say you steal every scene you're in.'

'Maybe that's why Marina's nose is out of joint.'

'Naughty, naughty, she is a little jealous, I suppose.' Liz broke off as the phone rang. They were sitting in Liz's office and the phone had rung for most of the morning. The media, people in the business, someone 'social' Liz had overlooked for the party.

'Liz Stoddart,' she clipped off crisply. 'Why Helen!' Her face and tone underwent a considerable change. 'How lovely to hear from you. Everything's arranged . . .' Liz paused while Helen spoke at the other end. 'Really, but that's awful! Poor darling. Oh, I am disappointed. Jane will be too. Both of us were so desperately wanting you to be with us. Yes, she's here now . . . yes . . . you will be able to make the first night? The invitations will go off again. And the plane tickets. No, it's all good . . . marvellous really . . . nothing but good news . . . the diaries? The greatest good fortune . . . all the difference in the world! . . . No, I never could become reconciled to the mystery

. . . yes, a marvellous scene. I doubt if there will be a dry eye in the house. Yes, he's fine . . . finished the novel. It speaks to me. It really does . . . No, I don't think so, Helen. I really treasure my independence . . . lovely . . . thank you, dear. I will . . . keep in touch.' Liz finished off and wriggled the receiver at Jane. 'Helen wants to talk to you. Unfortunately they can't make it.'

Helen's voice at the other end was as warm as ever. Robert had gone down with a virus which he had ignored until it put him into hospital for a few days with complications. They were both deeply disappointed they wouldn't be able to fly down. Everything, in fact, had been arranged. Air tickets, a chauffeur-driven Rolls to meet them at the airport and drive to their hotel where flowers and champagne had been placed in their suite. The studio had turned on the treatment but one couldn't count on anything going to plan. Alex, of course, was a very special guest, but Alex was in Rome.

'He wants to bring Bella home,' Helen told Jane excitedly. 'And she wants to come. It will be wonderful! In a sense Bella has been an exile.'

They spoke for several more minutes before Helen, promising to give their love to Robert, rang off.

'Why, oh, why, did that have to happen?' Liz wailed. 'I was so counting on some members of the family to come. Alex would knock 'em all dead, but formidable old Alex is in Rome. God, he's a complicated man! Whatever went wrong between you two? I would have thought you were insanely in love. Didn't he guard you like the crown jewels? Every time he looked at you didn't it make even my old knees tremble? I thought he was keeping himself on a pretty tight leash. Alex is the kind of man who just takes what he wants and we all knew he wanted you. So what happened?'

'Maybe his passion for me burned out.'

'I doubt it.' Liz pulled a face.

'Maybe he blames me for his grandmother's sudden death.'

'Darling!' Liz looked directly into Jane's huge, glittering eyes. 'You're talking nonsense and you know it. It's my belief the old ... lady just decided to die just as she decided everything else. You're simply not to blame for anything though you've heaped plenty on yourself.'

'I was the one who caused her plans to go astray,' Jane insisted. 'Maybe if I'd never gone to Monteverdi Alex would have married Antonella.'

'Well, he could have done, I suppose, but it would never have lasted. Granted she's gorgeous and I dare say that would turn any man's head, for a time. But Alex is too clever and complex. He has a very highly developed personality. He has so much personal charm and I know he detested Antonella's unkindnesses to the staff. However fond of her he was because of their long-standing relationship, she was as nothing compared to you. The old lady encouraged her to believe Alex might marry her. It was cruel and very wrong.'

'He made love to her.'

'That's what bothers me. It would be hard to forget Alex's lovemaking, but I guess you can't expect a man to marry all the women he's made love to. I mean what's the limit? Alex loved you, Jane. No question about that and he's a very positive man. Are you sure you didn't turn your back on him?'

'Never!' Jane, reed-slender, sprang up and paced the room. 'It was Alex who became so remote.'

'You both did,' Liz maintained. 'The Signora's

death took us all that way. I, for one, was glad the shooting was almost over.' Liz went to Jane and put her hand on her shoulder. 'Listen, sweetie, take some advice from an old maid. Don't let misunderstandings stand in your way. Talk it out. Silence is a dangerous thing, I've always found. Perhaps Alex feels he would be robbing you of a career. Perry did his best to give him that impression. In fact Perry told one or two wicked lies.'

'I don't want a career, Liz.' Jane lifted the single string of pearls she wore at her throat. 'It's an exciting world but there's quite a price to be paid. I know it seemed I had considerable talent for the part but would you believe me if I told you I was being directed? Not by Perry. I always gave Perry what he wanted but he never really showed me how. I *was* Laura Hamilton for a time.'

'Yes, you were.' Liz put her arm around Jane and hugged her. 'Equally, I believe, like Perry, you could have a big future.'

'As a wife and mother most of all. That's what I really want, Liz. Lots of love in my life. Fame and fortune couldn't lure me away from it. The most glamorous public life couldn't compensate for a barren home-life and that seems to be the way of it—most of the time.'

'Perry was hoping to talk you into going back with him,' Liz said in some depression.

'He's already spoken to me.' Jane picked up her soft leather handbag.

'Recently?' Liz gave her a direct frown.

'A few days ago.'

'Okay, so he's going to offer you the starring role in his new movie.'

'I wouldn't take it.'

'You haven't heard it yet.'

'Oh, Liz, darling, you really haven't been in love.'
Jane eyes were so blinded by tears she could hardly
see. 'All I want is *Alex*.'

In the end, Jane wore an extravagantly beautiful
creation in magnolia silk. It was the inspiration of a
dazzling young designer, Camilla Preston, and it
captured the romantic mood of the film. The bodice
was tight and low-cut with exceptionally beautiful
bouffant sleeves: the tiny waist was sashed in a subtle
shade of green satin, enhancing the green of Jane's
eyes, and the skirt, using masses and masses of
material, billowed like a ballgown.

'Straight out of *Gone with the Wind*,' Bryan said
when he saw her.

'*Prisoner of the Sun*, don't you mean, darling?' Liz
was resplendent in shot plum-silk brocade.

Everyone who was anyone had turned up and the
women were dressed in a wonderful mixture of
fabrics: lace, silk, satin, black georgette, tons of
sequins and glitter, anything that was glamorous,
luxurious, eye-catching, a provocative show of bosoms,
high-cut splits that showed long slender legs, all the
really serious jewellery and a lot of *trompe-l'oeil*. It was
a truly glittering occasion and all the guests had
polished themselves up like jewels.

None was more flawless than Jane.

Only selected guests had been asked to the sneak
preview and the comments afterwards were not only
wholly reassuring but little short of ecstatic.

'It's a long time since I've enjoyed myself so much,'
a leading critic told Liz. 'Very good, darling. Very
good indeed. The little Gilmour is a wonderful find.
She is a very, very beautiful Laura. Small wonder our
Perry is so obsessed with her!'

At one point Jane found herself a virtual prisoner of

excited fans. She couldn't possibly snub them yet a weak feeling of claustrophobia was overcoming her. Obviously, unlike Marina and David, who were loving it, she didn't belong to this world; the barrage of questions, comments, the avid glances. She was public property.

The agitation that was growing in her, causing her cheeks to flush and her green eyes to go huge and glittery, engaged the attention of a tall, handsome, dark-haired man who broke away from a group who were demanding information and headed straight for her.

'Excuse me, please?'

By virtue of his height and lean, powerful strength he had little difficulty parting the thick crowd, taking Jane's arm and drawing her unhurriedly but purposely away from the throng.

'Alex, oh my God, am I pleased to see you.'

'Terrify you, do they, darling?' His blue eyes were as brilliant, as mocking as ever. 'You looked like the princess in a fairy-tale beset by the rabble.'

'I had no idea you were going to be here.'

'Nothing like surprises.'

She stared almost dazedly at his handsome profile. 'Does Liz know you're here? Perry, the others?'

'Liz does.' He nodded his dark head. 'The others, I don't know. I haven't given it much thought. The only one I'm interested in is you.'

'I don't know that I can handle it,' her green eyes flashed, 'I certainly haven't been on your mind the past few months.'

Liz was rushing towards them, arms stretched out.

'Alex, how absolutely marvellous! You made it!'

'You knew and you didn't tell me?' Jane looked at her friend in dismay.

'Don't blame me, sweetie,' Liz defended herself. 'Alex was very definite and he's a very definite man.'

'Just the same . . .' Jane nibbled her soft underlip.

Perry, his smooth face almost radiant, broke the grip of a statuesque woman who couldn't seem to stop hugging him and hurried over.

'Alex, what a happy occasion!' He shook hands. 'I'm so sorry the rest of the family couldn't come.'

'They'll make it the next time, I promise,' Alex returned smoothly. 'Congratulations, I enjoyed the film immensely as did everyone else judging from the reaction. It was a moving experience reliving the McGovern saga the way it was meant to be told.'

'Congratulate Jane!' Perry insisted, turning to Jane and staring at her with voracious eyes. 'She was the one who really brought those diaries to light. You were wonderful tonight, Jane. Absolutely pure, sweet, convincing. A most difficult role and you carried it off. I found myself staring at you . . . *staring* at you. It's virtually impossible for the camera to find less than a perfect angle. I've so many plans to outline to you later on.'

'Did you hear that, Jane?' Alex said suavely.

'I suggest we move on now,' Liz urged. 'Crowds always make me a bit nervous and we're packed out tonight.'

The party was held at the harbourside mansion of Lady Gower, probably the most celebrated patroness of the arts in the whole country and certainly the richest. It was the Gower mansion that had been used for certain scenes in the film and Lady Gower, like the McGoverns, had been a major investor.

As soon as she found out who Alex was, she whisked him off to be introduced to her dearest friends, and Jane found herself the centre of ever-changing, admiring circles. Because he was so tall—apart from being far too handsome—she never lost track of Alex.

Once she saw Marina throw her arms around his neck and kiss him—much as a woman would her long-lost favourite lover—despite the fact her balding rich husband rarely moved from her elbow. Susan Ransom, who had been recently elevated to the status of David Breeden's fiancée, for her part rarely took her eyes off Jane as though convinced there had been something between David and his co-star that positively needed discouraging, until she happened to intercept a glance between Jane and Alex McGovern. It was so emotion-charged that Susan, feeling a little breathless, immediately relaxed. She hadn't been able to stand the thought of David's being interested in anyone else, now she felt amazed she hadn't known. If anyone looked at her the way Alex McGovern looked at Jane, she would blush.

The party followed the usual pattern. Lots of talk and drink and afterwards a superb supper, where guests served themselves from candle-lit, flower-decked long tables, then moved to set tables that had been arranged around a magnificent courtyard and pool area.

Jane was so churned up she wasn't hungry, though the tables were piled with a sumptuous spread of food, and magnums of champagne ran like water. Perry had attached himself to her almost gloatingly, seemingly unable to credit Jane didn't need all the adulation as he did. There was great pleasure in being told she looked beautiful or her performance had been most moving but her ego didn't soak it all up like a sponge. Neither was she a true party girl. She only wanted one man, not dozens of men appraising her face and her body, wondering what she'd be like to make love to. Sincerity was everything when so much of the talk seemed feigned.

By one o'clock in the morning Jane desperately

wanted to leave. Liz and Bryan were having one of their good nights together, Perry was an insomniac anyway and hours later the women couldn't take their eyes off Alex. He gave every appearance of having a wonderful time until Jane moved towards her hostess, then it appeared he had had quite enough.

'I'm taking Jane home, Lady Gower,' he explained smoothly, looking down at his hostess and giving her his heart-stopping smile. 'Thank you for inviting me to your beautiful home. Remember when you're in our part of the world you must come to us.'

'Oh, I must, I must!' Lady Gower gazed up at him, dazzled. 'I simply must see you again. You too, Jane,' she turned and purred. 'You look enchanting in that magical dress. Are you sure you can't stay a little bit longer? Lots of my guests stay to breakfast.'

Jane declined as pleasantly as she knew how. A lot of the guests seemed hell-bent on getting themselves drunk!

'You don't have to come with me,' Jane said when they were out in the drive.

'I swear I'll go crazy if I have to go back inside.'

'Really?' Jane followed when he led. 'I thought you were having a marvellous time.'

'Fending off all those nymphomaniacs?'

'You really are rather splendid. It's not every day a girl gets a chance to break loose. What's next on the agenda, a night-club?'

'Your place, I think. I don't want to take you back to the hotel.'

'You surely don't think I'm going to invite you in?'

'That's exactly what you're going to do.'

'For more of your exquisite games of domination?'

'Hush,' he said quietly. 'You're a bundle of nerves.'

Jane, since she had been earning so much more money, lived in a spacious sun-filled unit in one of

Sydney's beautiful harbourside suburbs. Apart from giving Alex directions and asking after Robert, who was much improved, she had little to say. She settled her beautifully coiffured blonde head back into the bucket seat of the hired Mercedes planning what she would say when he began to assert his dark mastery. At Monteverdi he had enslaved her, then treated her as if she didn't exist for long months. Pride demanded that this time he was going to come off the worse.

At her door she silently passed him her keys, glancing coolly at his dark gold profile. She had never seen him in evening-dress before and she almost gave way under the impact of his sheer male beauty. It was difficult to say which emotion was the more fierce, pride or passion. This was the first time they had been alone all night, the first time in hungry months. Despite herself as she took the keys back her fingers were shaking. Desire was like a storm. It built up slowly to a point when she could not withstand it.

He moved around the open-plan living-dining-room, switching on lights, then he went to the sliding glass doors leading on to the small plant-filled balcony and opened one door to admit the cool night breeze.

'Make yourself at home,' Jane said laconically.

'I'm determined to.' There was a mocking curve to his chiselled lips. 'You're an enchantress tonight, Jane. I've never seen you look more lovely and that's the most enchanting dress. Innocent seduction, delicacy, refinement. You shone as Laura Hamilton.'

'But I'm not so captivating as myself?'

'However would you think that?' He locked her with his eyes.

'Would you care for something to drink?' She turned abruptly, putting her evening-bag down on a small side-table. 'I suppose not, after that party.'

'Actually I didn't drink much at all.' He moved

backwards and slumped very elegantly into a green velvet-upholstered armchair. 'I don't really need it, you know.'

'I'm glad. I rather detest too much.'

'It would be marvellous if you would just sit down. Over here, near me. I want to look at you. God, how I want to look at you. I want to see the light pooling over your hair and skin and that gorgeous dress. You really could become a screen idol, if you liked.'

'So Perry keeps saying.' His words, the look in his brilliant eyes, everything about him kept throwing her off balance. She sank down into the armchair opposite him with her magnificent magnolia skirt spreading out like the giant creamy petals of the grandiflora. Her hair glinted like gold and the skin of her face and throat and the slight downward curve of her exposed breasts was like cream.

'And has he succeeded in convincing you? You're very talented, you know that? You could go a long way. It could be very hard for you to deny yourself a career.'

'Certainly,' she only allowed herself to look up at him briefly, 'if that's what I wanted.'

'You could make a great deal of money.'

'Even for the rich money can be a problem. Money isn't the big thing in my life, Alex.'

'Unlike a lot of females. I've been worshipped, for my money.'

'You might think that. I think they probably loved you.'

'Well, do you blame me then if it nagged at my mind? Being rich, very rich isn't all that easy. It can defeat you, if you don't put more back into life than you take out. You're different, Gianina, from anyone I have ever known. You're the only woman who hasn't given a damn about my money or how much you can make for yourself either. You're very clear-eyed. You have a true set of values.'

'Thank you. I'll sleep on that,' she said wryly. 'Helen told me you went to Rome to see your mother.'

'I did and what is more, I've brought her home.' His blue eyes blazed into hers. I want my mother to enjoy her life. She has not been happy. I want her to be able to nurse her first grandchild.'

'I can understand that,' Jane said gravely, 'but do you intend to get married first?'

'But I have chosen my wife already.'

'Did you remember to ask her first?' Jane's large green eyes glittered. 'I have a grudging admiration for your male arrogance but it does limit a woman to a certain role.'

'Wouldn't *you* like to marry me?'

The light gleamed on the sudden flush on her cheeks. 'Is that a proposal or are you gauging reactions?'

'You won't stop fighting me, will you?' He moved very swiftly, going on his knees before her and placing his two hands on her tiny waist. 'I would give up everything in the world for you, Gianina, if you asked me to.'

'Alex, please. I don't know what you're saying.'

'I love you. There's no other woman in the world for me. There never has been. Never will be.'

'But you let me go?'

He moved his hands very gently to beneath her breasts. 'My love, you left and I took a gamble that might have destroyed me.'

'Why?' For the first time she bent towards him with her mouth parted.

'Why?' His laugh was short, almost savage. He threw her up like a doll and carried her to a long built-in sofa piled up with cushions. 'Because I have to allow you a choice. You have real talent, real beauty. How can I deny you your accomplishments? You could have all of it. Money, marriage, a career. I couldn't *persuade* you into marrying me, trick you, use emotional blackmail. Hell, I could, I suppose. But I love you, Gianina.'

'Did you need to torture me to prove it?'

She only saw the brilliant flash of his eyes before he brought down his mouth with such crushing pressure that she gave a strangled moan of defeat and desire.

'Alex . . .'

'Stop talking . . . stop thinking . . . I *want* you.'

'And I want *you*.' Why should she be afraid to admit it?

'Do you . . . *do* you?' His mouth craved hers, the satiny feel of her skin. 'I've had a demon driving me all night. Do you know that? I wanted to pick you up and simply carry you off. I wanted to take you away from that life. From Wyndham and men like him. It's a terrible experience watching other men devour you with their eyes. It must happen to these love-goddesses. I can't even think they enjoy it. The only happiness is in something lasting.'

'It's all right, Alex darling.' She tried to calm him. 'I love you. Only you. There must be some way I can show you how much.'

'You can show me how much you want me—in bed. You can show me how much you love me by marrying me. Now.'

'Tonight?' She was experiencing a high of exultation.

'You want a big wedding don't you? I have brought my beautiful mother home. She is longing to meet you, longing to love you. There will never be a conflict such as there was with Nonna. In any case my mother wants her own home. I have promised her the home that she yearns for, not huge and grand but something more simple and lovely that complements her personality.'

'You're a good son,' Jane said softly, something that enhanced him in her eyes.

'I'll be a better husband,' he told her almost fiercely. 'Gianina, little one, do you think I can get you out of that dress? I want so much to make love to you and it's so beautiful I don't want to crush it.' Even as he was begging her, characteristically he had taken the initiative, unzipping the magnolia silk and lifting it away from her warm, trembling body.

'God, you're beautiful, beautiful . . .' The words escaped him in a groan. 'Tell me, Gianina, what is it you want of me?'

'Your mind, body and soul.'

'You have that.' He bent his head and kissed her breast. 'But have you decided on a career? Monteverdi is isolated and I can't pretend that I could leave it, all the time. It needs me.'

She arched her slender body beneath his caressing hands. 'You and me on an island would be enough. I was meant to come to Monteverdi, Alex, meant to play Laura Hamilton. It is the only role I ever wish to play. You are everything I've been searching for. You, our children, our life. I couldn't ask for a more beautiful part of the world. Paradise. You mean you allowed me to think your love for me had burned out, when you were waiting for me to make a choice?'

'Love never burns out, Gianina.' He pulled her close up against him and buried his face in her hair. 'Oh, God, what torment these last months have been. I was terrified I would break out and force you to become part of me. I wouldn't even allow you to argue. I am used to having my way.'

'Darling, I know that.'

'You're sure?' He bent her back with savage tenderness.

'Sure?' She lifted her arm rhythmically, letting her fingers caress the nape of his neck. 'My love, it's my dream.'

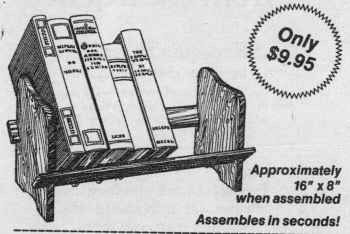

Six exciting series for you every month... from Harlequin

Harlequin Romance
The series that started it all

Tender, captivating and heartwarming...
love stories that sweep you off to faraway places
and delight you with the magic of love.

Harlequin Presents
Powerful contemporary love stories...as individual as the women who read them

The No. 1 romance series...
exciting love stories for you, the woman of today...
a rare blend of passion and dramatic realism.

Harlequin Superromance
It's more than romance... it's Harlequin Superromance

A sophisticated, contemporary romance-fiction
series, providing you with a longer,
more involving read...a richer mix of complex plots,
realism and adventure.

Harlequin
American Romance
Harlequin celebrates the American woman...

...by offering you romance stories written about American women, by American women for American women. This series offers you contemporary romances uniquely North American in flavor and appeal.

◆

Harlequin Temptation
Passionate stories for today's woman

An exciting series of sensual, mature stories of love...dilemmas, choices, resolutions... all contemporary issues dealt with in a true-to-life fashion by some of your favorite authors.

◆

Harlequin Intrigue
Because romance can be quite an adventure

Harlequin Intrigue, an innovative series that blends the romance you expect... with the unexpected. Each story has an added element of intrigue that provides a new twist to the Harlequin tradition of romance excellence.

Harlequin Books

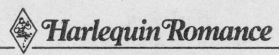

Harlequin Romance

Coming Next Month

2821 ROAD TO LOVE Katherine Arthur
A free-lance photographer happens upon a Clark Gable
look-alike and a chance to pay off her debts. So when he takes
off across America in his shiny silver semi, little does he know
she's along for the ride.

2822 THE FOLLY OF LOVING Catherine George
Times are tough, and it seems foolhardy for an Englishwoman
to turn down a famous actor's marriage proposal. But he broke
her heart eight years ago. So hasn't he done enough already?

2823 WINTER AT WHITECLIFFS Miriam Macgregor
The owner of Whitecliffs sheep station in New Zealand puts
his ward's tutor on a month's trial, and all because he thinks
she's after his half brother. But if he knew where her true
interests lay...

2824 THE SECRET POOL Betty Neels
A nurse's holiday in Holland seems the perfect escape from the
critical appraisal of a certain Dutch doctor—until he tracks her
down, having decided she's perfect for a particular job after all.

2825 RUDE AWAKENING Elizabeth Power
A computer programmer, accused by her suspicious-minded
boss of stealing company secrets, finds herself kept prisoner by
him until she can prove her innocence.

2826 ROUGH DIAMOND Kate Walker
The volatile attraction a young Englishwoman felt for her rebel
from the wrong side of the tracks is reignited years later—along
with the doubts and confusion that drove them apart.

Available in March wherever paperback books are sold, or
through Harlequin Reader Service.

In the U.S.
P.O. Box 1397
Buffalo, N.Y.
14240-1397

In Canada
P.O. Box 603
Fort Erie, Ontario
L2A 5X3